BALDILOCKS

AND THE THREE DARES

BALDILOCKS
AND
THE THREE DARES

BY
JIMOTHY NEWTON

Design and illustrations by Tricia Seibold

Yudu Studios
Menlo Park, CA

First Printing, 2017
17 18 19 20 21   10 9 8 7 6 5 4 3 2 1

ISBN 978-0-9987076-2-4
ISBN 978-0-9987076-3-1 (hc)
ISBN 978-0-9987076-4-8 (eb)
ISBN 978-0-9987076-5-5 (ab)

Library of Congress Control Number: 2017944425

Edited by Allister Thompson
Design and illustration by Tricia Seibold

Published by Yudu Studios 2017
Menlo Park, California, USA

For information about bulk purchases, sales promotions,
fund-raising and educational needs, contact Yudu Studios at
1-650-761-2253 or info@yudustudios.com.

Find us at
baldilocks3dares.org/the-book
and
facebook.com/groups/baldilocks3dares

Teacher resources including notes and blackline masters can
be found at baldilocks3dares.org/teachers

All proceeds from the sale of *Baldilocks and the Three Dares*
go to the following children's charities: Dreamflight
(dreamflight.org), MDA (mda.org), SNAP (snapkids.org),
and Solving Kids' Cancer (solvingkidscancer.org).

For more information, please visit *baldilocks3dares.org*

To Kira and all of the amazing, inspirational kids of
Dreamflight (dreamflight.org)
MDA summer camp (mda.org)
SNAP (snapkids.org)
Solving Kids' Cancer (solvingkidscancer.org)

CONTENTS

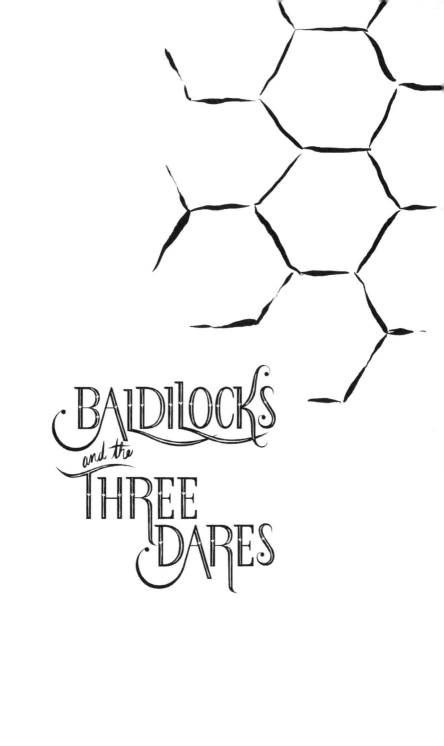

BALDILOCKS

and the

THREE DARES

THE MAKING OF BALDILOCKS:
AN AUTHOR'S NOTE

For the past fifteen years I have had the honor and joy of working, playing, and generally goofing off with a group of incredible kids, all battling serious, chronic, and life-threatening health issues. *Baldilocks and the Three Dares* is a labor of love meant to honor the courage, compassion, and endless sense of humor they display every day. Ideally, it will inspire the rest of us to be just a little more like them.

I was particularly moved by Kira, an amazing thirteen-year old girl from Edinburgh, Scotland, who loves WWE wrestling, doing a little "Lean and Dab" with friends, and who happens to be battling neuroblastoma…for the second time. We met through Dreamflight, an equally amazing organization that takes kids with serious illnesses or disabilities on a ten-day journey of fun and self-discovery—one that pushes boundaries, empowers, and builds self-esteem.

Baldilocks and the Three Dares came to life under an apple tree on a farm in central Oregon, where I spent the summer talking to cows, bees, snakes (and any other critter that wandered by), and scribbling away in my two-dollar spiral notebook. The result is the book in your hand, something that gives me great pride but is quite different from the book I originally set out to write. This was supposed to be a small, thirty-two-page children's picture book, à la Seuss. That changed pretty quickly. No sooner had I parked myself in that pasture, surrounded by the wonders of Animalia, than the story quickly morphed into a much bigger middle-grade chapter book. It also, of course, switched from having humans as the main characters to animals. I blame the farm...and my fondness for character development.

Speaking of book transformation: as you will notice, *Baldilocks and the Three Dares* starts in verse and then transitions to prose. This serves as a nice metaphor for the childhood-to-teenage transition. The order, consistency, and purity of youth—looked after, protected, and sheltered—suddenly becomes the more random, unpredictable, harsh world of young adulthood.

Regardless of format, my hope is that you will feel a connection to one or more of the characters and follow along as they discover that despite life's adversities and our own imperfections—as daunting as they may be—there is always a path forward. *Baldilocks and the Three Dares* is ultimately a story of overcoming our inner demons and some of life's biggest challenges by discovering that life is a team sport. We can't prevent or even get rid of life's challenges, but there is a way through...together.

DEPARTURE

Four tiny pink feet scurried across the linoleum. A light *clickety-click* could be heard as the nails repeatedly hit the shiny surface, failing to get traction. More clicks and a longer scratch as the feet passed between a bright pink pair of Crocs, sliding to a stop just under the privacy curtain.

His chest heaved as he tried to catch his breath before the next dash. Heart pounding, he turned back toward the bed and looked up one last time to see her beautiful smiley face. *Move along*, she gestured, tears rolling down her cheeks. *Go on now. Go!*

Suddenly, the Crocs moved. "Hey…what the—I told you, you can't have him in here! Get that mouse outta here!"

A year earlier…

"Oh, come on, Mom! How am I supposed to make that kind of decision?" she said.

"I know, I know, sweetie. But here's the thing, sometimes—"

"Sometimes we have to make tough choices…and none of the choices are fun…blah, blah, blah…" she mocked.

"No…no," Mom bluffed defiantly, "that is not what I was going to say."

Her daughter rolled her eyes. "Oh, really?" she said. "Please, do tell. What *is* it then, you were going to say? Sometimes…"

Mom looked determined. "Sometimes…" she replied, fumbling for words. "Sometimes…all your choices just—" She paused, pacing back and forth, looking increasingly frustrated. "They all suck!" Both froze, jaws hanging open… then burst into laughter.

"You said suck!" her daughter said.

"I did not," Mom argued, a small grin forming at the corners of her mouth.

"You did!"

"Yeah, yeah," Mom said, waving her hands about as she tried to distract and get things back on topic. "The point is…you still have to make the tough choices. You have to push yourself."

"I know, Mom, I know!"

"Just make a game out of it or something. Come on. I *dare* you."

Her brother suddenly barged into the room. "And I double dare you!"

"Kyle, we are having a talk," Mom said.

"No, no, it's fine." His sister grinned. "Come on in. We are having a talk *break* just now." Mom rolled her eyes.

"Oh, good," he said as he walked over to her bed, "I have something for you." From his right hand dangled a small brown paper bag with twine handles…and it seemed to be making a sound…a scratchy sound. It was moving!

"AAAGH, get that away from me! What is it?" his sister yelled.

"Kyle!" Mom said. "Stop exciting your sister. She's supposed to be resting."

Curious, his sister gingerly reached out and took the bag. "If this is a giant spider, I am going to kill you." She slowly opened the top, carefully peeking one eye over the edge of the bag. "Eww, what is it?" She jiggled the bag a bit to get it to move, but it just flopped over. "Is it dead? Thanks a lot. Thanks for the dead…uh…whatever it is."

"It's not dead. He's just a heavy…napper."

"It looks like a deformed eraser…with feet."

"It's a baby mouse! I was going to feed him to my snake but—"

"What?"

"Pick him up. He's really soft and rubbery."

She gently reached down, plucked the small bundle of pink flesh from the bottom of the bag, and held him in her palm. "Awww," both she and Mom muttered.

Reaching down with a finger, she ever so carefully tried to pet his head without crushing him. One knuckle on her tiniest finger was still twice as big as his whole body. "He is so cute! Can I keep him?" she said. "Please?"

Her mother watched in amazement as this wee creature had an almost instant calming effect on her daughter…so much so that she was actually starting to fall asleep as she stroked his tiny head and back. "Of course you can, honey. You absolutely can keep him." Mom gestured to Kyle to head for the door. "Come on," she whispered, "Let's let her slee—"

"Ahem," she interrupted. "Where are you going? I believe at least one of you—Kyle—owes me a bedtime story."

"Is it my turn again already?" he mumbled.

"And this time make it one of those ones that starts with a rhyme. You know, like Mom and Dad used to read to us when we were kids."

"What? Like Goldilocks and the Three Bears or something?

"That doesn't rhy—" she started to say as a big yawn suddenly took over. "UUHHHH." Her eyes were starting to droop even as she spoke. "Oh, and make sure you do all the voices. I love it when you do the voices."

"But I didn't bring any books," he said.

"Just make one up…" Another, even bigger yawn caught her midsentence, causing both Kyle and Mom to yawn as well. "…like you always do." Mom nodded encouragingly.

"Alright," he grumbled, scooting a large, cushy chair alongside her bed. "But you have to promise to go to sleep."

"Already there, big brother. Already th…" And so it began.

CHAPTER 1

MORNING NEW

Gooooood morning…is a phrase that I do
With the emphasis placed on the "oooooo."
It is something I say,
As the night turns to day,
And I'm ready to try something new.

Which is just how it started with Kee,
A most playful and wee honeybee.
She started alone,
Neither worker nor drone,
'Til she took on a dare…no wait, three!

As with all bees, maintaining your hive,
Is that which you do to survive.
But one day while she slept,
A bad creeper had crept,
And creeped off with a wing on one side.

That morning she woke same as most,
Had a yawn then a piece of bee toast.
Put her stinger on tight,
And then reached to her right,
Where she'd hung both her wings on a post.

Now Kee was not known for her sight.
She wore glasses all day, then at night.
But still it was clear,
There was just one wing here,
And she yelled a great yell, "Where's my right?!"

In a panic she buzzed to and fro,
Searching each bunk above then below.
Every bunk in the hive,
Fifty thousand and five,
But no luck, she broke down and cried, "NO!"

In a list of cry types, there are seven,
From "Ouch, that hurt," to "Oh my heaven!"
But in tears-by-the-pail,
On a 1 to 10 scale,
Poor Kee was quite clearly eleven.

She cried 'til she filled up her bed
And soaked every hair on her head.
Oh the water did flow,
Down to each bunk below,
'Til every last tear had been shed.

Now, the nice thing about a good cry—
It does much more than just cleanse the eye.
Your worries and scaries,
Those brain dingleberries,
Are less dingly, though not quite sure why.

Still, that night, oh the thoughts that were thunk,
Couldn't sleep, Kee snuck out of her bunk.
Down the ladder with ease,
While her bunkmates made zzzz's,
Out the door, face-to-face with a skunk!

CHAPTER 2

YOU DON'T STINK

As every nose knows, skunks are stinkers,
Prolific in "pew," not as thinkers.
But Kyle was a little bit
Caught in the middle, it seems,
Like a car with both blinkers.

Thus that meeting when skunk first met bee,
Did not go as usually.
Instead of the deal,
Where bee becomes meal,
Kyle stopped when he heard, "Hi, I'm Kee!"

Though still dark, he could just now make out
A wee shape, near his nose, came a shout,
"Could you give me a ride?"
"I've no wing on one side."
And with that she jumped onto his snout.

For a minute or two they just stared,
One eyes crossed and the other eyes flared!
Both tried not to blink,
Or to make a big stink,
Then, "I'm Kyle. Come along…if you dare!"

Kee grinned and turned 'round on Kyle's nose,
Waving "bye" to the hive and corn rows.
Confused by this chummy bee,
Not in his tummy,
He walked on, just to see where this goes.

Her excitement, she could hardly keep in,
Lots of questions, but where to begin.
"Why aren't you smelly?"
"Or you in my belly?"
Replied he quite snidely with a grin.

Yes, yes, you admit, this is strange!
Let me guess, you just wanted a change.
Taste of bee is blasé,
And perfume's what I spray,
Is that it or some form of derange?

Ooh, how about this…
Home, home of derange…get it?
Wait, wait…uhhh…
Where the traveling mates are so strange…
Uh…an intelligent bee
Rides across the prairie
On a skunk that's less stunk and more mange…

"Enough!" Kyle yelled, sounding shaken.

"What? Sorry, just messin' around. You know, mixin' things up…"

"Quiet," he whispered, coming to a sudden stop.

"Really, I was just—" she began, but Kyle quickly covered her up with his paw, almost smashing her against his nose.

She felt the rise and fall of his nostrils with her feet. His quickening pulse passed straight from the pad of his paw to the hairs on her head. *Predator*, she thought. *But what kind of creature considers a stinky skunk a meal?*

"Use your stink," she murmured, hoping he would somehow get the message. *Just use it! Why isn't he—*

"Hang on!" he whispered, and then *whoosh!* The next thing she knew, she was clinging to the hairs on his nose as he bolted into the woods.

It was quite dark now, so she could hardly see anything but the rapid splash of shadows. Kyle was zigging and zagging so fast, Kee was sure she'd be thrown any moment.

"Aaaaaagh," she yelled as another sharp turn almost tossed her off his snout. She wasn't sure but seemed to be just dangling from Kyle's upper lip.

Then, as quickly as he had started, Kyle suddenly stopped, put a paw up to Kee, hesitated for just a moment, and pushed her into his mouth.

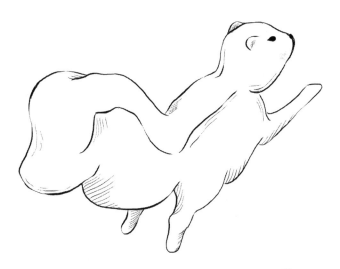

CHAPTER 3

ODDBALLS

I t was warm, dark, and gooey...and the smell, oh my, the smell! "Now I know where all the stink comes from," Kee mumbled. "I always thought it was the other end!"

Between the smell, the goo, and the nearly constant squeeze between tongue and the roof of his mouth, it was all she could do to resist her instinct to sting. Occasionally the squeeze would let up. Then, just for a moment, she would slide—well, it was more of a slosh, actually—from one side of his mouth to the other, slam up against a cheek, and come to a sudden stop, squeezed from the top and bottom. Without thinking, she would lift her abdomen into position, ready to drive her stinger into his tongue, but then catch herself. "Don't make me use this," she grumbled.

Meanwhile, Kyle was off again, dashing through trees and over rocks, all the while inflating his mouth like a balloon in an attempt not to chomp down on his wee passenger. He zigged left, then right. Seeing a small outcropping in the hillside below, he ducked in behind, came to a stop, and spat a saliva-covered bee-ball into his paw.

"Blech," he said, squinting, snout scrunched like an accordion. "Disgusting!" His tongue dangled out of the side of his mouth, a stream of drool making a tiny waterfall onto his belly. "No offense," he continued, using his other paw to scrape the excess bee taste off his tongue. "There's just something about bee that—" He stopped, noticing that Kee wasn't moving.

"Kee?" he called, shaking his paw a bit. No response. "Kee!" More forcefully now, poking her with his other paw. He blew on her a few times, trying to dry her off, but still nothing. "Kee!" he yelled, nudging her with his nose. "Come on, stop goofing off," he said, sounding more and more desperate. Shaken, he gently set her down on a nearby rock and stepped back, staring. "What have I done?" he mumbled to himself. "What am I doing? She's just a bee. She's just a bee!" He bent down and nudged her one more time with his nose, but no movement. He picked her up and placed her gently back onto his snout. "Oh, Kee," he sighed. Then, in a last bit of frustration, he shook his head. "KEE!"

Her wing fluttered slightly, but he wasn't sure if it was just the wind. Suddenly she shook, sprang up, and immediately pointed her stinger straight down, ready to plunge. "Yes!" Kyle said with glee. "You're okay. You're okay!" Then he noticed the stinger. "Wait, wait…NO!"

Kee, suddenly aware of what she was about to do, snapped out of it and stopped herself.

"Whew, that was close!" Kyle said. "I thought I had squished you." Kee, feeling it was indeed a little too close, decided to make him squirm a bit and lowered her abdomen ever closer to his tender nose. A look of angry determination suddenly washed over her face. "Noooo!" Kyle yelled.

"Why…why shouldn't I?" she said, still a bit dazed. "Maybe you deserve a little anguish."

"No!" Kyle yelled again, shaking his head.

"It won't kill you."

"Yes, I know," he said, "but won't it kill you?"

Kee thought for a moment, then her face took on a look of acceptance. "Oh, right. Good point. Truce?"

"Uh, sure," he said, not having thought they were in a fight in the first place.

Kee looked around, regaining her bearings. "So, I guess we outran him?" Kyle realized he had forgotten all about the threat, too worried about crushing Kee.

He put a paw up to his mouth. "Shhhh." He sniffed around for any signs of trouble.

"Why didn't you just stinkify him?" Kee said, still annoyed.

"Shhhh!"

"I mean, seriously. You almost killed us both with all your running around," she continued. Kyle scanned the horizon but saw nothing. "I mean a simple spray…how hard is it to…"

Kyle suddenly shot Kee a look of contempt, less

concerned now with an external threat and more with the one currently nagging at him from his snout.

"Wait…wait a minute," Kee said in sudden realization, pointing a tiny bee leg at his big eyes. "That's it! That's it, isn't it? You *can't* stink! You're a skunk who can't *stink!* A skunk with no stunk," she exclaimed with excitement. "*That* is why I couldn't smell anything on you!" she mumbled. "I knew something was weird about—" She caught herself, seeing the defeat in Kyle's eyes as he sat down on his tail. "Wait, wait…it's okay," she tried to reassure him. "Don't you see," she said with a big grin, "you're…" She gulped, a little bit choked up for a second. "You're like me! We're the same," she added, waving her one wing excitedly. "We're both oddballs!" Kyle closed his eyes and turned his head, trying to look away…forgetting she was actually attached to his head now. "We're different…so what?" she continued, with a new sense of hope and determination.

Kyle, listening now, slightly opened one eye, trying to do so without her seeing. Kee, practically sitting on his eyelash, noticed immediately, grabbed the lid, and did a full overhead press, pushing up with all her might. "Yoo-hoo," she said gleefully, waving her one wing as she stared into his big eye. "Anybody in there?" Kyle slammed his eye closed, knocking her on her back. From there she could now see a drop forming in the corner of his eye. It quickly started to grow and then released, rushing by, almost knocking her off his nose.

She climbed up his snout, between his two eyes, and down to his left ear. From there she felt the stuttered shake of a concealed cry trying to find its way out. Through her highly sensitive antennae, she could smell the saline of his tears starting to flow. She felt bad, knowing too well how he was feeling—different…damaged.

She crawled up to the edge of his big, hairy ear—at least it seemed big to her—and leaned in. "If it makes you feel any better," she whispered, "your *breath*…is disgusting!" He gave a half laugh, half cry kind of chuckle. Kee smiled. "I'm not kidding," she said as he sniffled and chuckled a little more. "I almost threw up all my honey!" Kyle laughed a little more. "I nearly stung you just to stop the misery. I briefly considered stinging myself!" Kyle was laughing out loud now. Soon he was chuckling with such force that Kee had to hang on just to keep from being thrown. "Woo-hoo, ride 'em cowboy!" she squealed with delight, gripping the tips of his ear with three feet while the other three waved wildly in the air like a cowgirl. Kyle got into the fun and started to gallop and kick like a bucking bronco, a big grin on his face. Unfortunately, Kyle was not particularly known for his coordination. He looked more like a rodent experiencing some kind of convulsions rather than a skunk trying to give a honeybee a ride. This went on for a while.

CHAPTER 4

GRUB RUSTLING

Precisely 25.2 seconds. That is apparently how long "a while" is when Kyle is bronco-bucking a honeybee. He fell in a lump of exhaustion with Kee tumbling back onto his chest. Still giggling, she threw herself onto her back, feet in the air, and now rode his rising and falling ribcage as he tried to catch his breath.

"Yeah, so there you have it," he was finally able to mutter, somewhat defeated. "I don't stink." Kee laughed. "It's not funny," he tried to insist before breaking down and giggling himself. "Alright, I guess it's a little funny. A skunk that can't stink." He shook his head. "At least *you* can defend yourself. You can sting!"

"Ha, right!" Kee said with a laugh. "As long as I happen to be already sitting *on top* of the culprit!" She waved her one wing. "Pardon me, Mr. Bear," she mocked from the end of his snout, "before you devour me and my hive, if you would be so kind as to pick me up and gently place me upon your nose." Kyle giggled. "Yes, yes, right there…the soft, tender part would be fine." Kyle snorted with delight, and a blackberry shot out his nose.

"When did I eat that?" he mumbled. Now Kee was rolling with laughter.

"Stop it, you're killing me!" She tumbled off his nose.

"Careful." He caught her at the last second and then set her gently on the ground. "Speaking of killing you…" he said with a grin.

"Yes, have you finally decided to eat me?"

"Not yet," he smiled, "but I'll think about it." Kee smiled back. "No…it's just that whole stinging thing. You only get one shot at it, right?" She squirmed a bit. "I mean, don't you die after you sting?" he pressed.

"Uh…I'd rather not talk about it," she replied. "You know what does kill me?" she quickly deflected. "Eating me!"

"Oh, not this again."

"But seriously, why didn't you eat me *and* the rest of the hive?" Kyle rolled his eyes and shook his head. "You knew we were all sleeping. You didn't even try! Do you really not like the taste of bees?"

Kyle thought for a second, then shook his head and shrugged. "No…no, I don't. You are all so fuzzy and… wingy…blech!" Kee laughed. "I tried. Heck, I was out there last night to try again," he said with a pause. "Until some crazy bee with only one wing jumps out of nowhere, straight onto my nose!" Kee giggled. "And then asks *me* for a ride! Who is going to take a chance with a nut like that? Likely toxic!" Kee giggled again.

"No," he continued, "what I like is a good grub...juicy, tender...and no after-sting!"

"Hee hee, good one," Kee snickered. She could suddenly feel the vibrations of Kyle's tummy rumbling far below. "Come on," she said. "Let's go get you some grub!"

Kyle put out a paw for Kee to climb on. He set her back on his nose, and she immediately started singing. "A-grubbin' we will go...a-grubbin' we will go... Hi-ho..." She paused and turned, waiting for Kyle to join in.

"Oh, right," he reluctantly responded. "Hi-ho the derry-o, a-grubbin' we will go."

Kyle pointed his snout in the air, sniffed around a few times, and then headed deeper into the woods. "So what does a grub smell like?" Kee asked. "Maybe I can help. These babies—" she wiggled her antennae "—make pretty good sniffers."

"Well," Kyle explained, "It's kind of a...musky smell... like a—" Just then there was a sound off to the left, and Kyle stopped. He started sniffing with his nose and Kee started probing the air with her antennae. It was now pitch dark. Kee couldn't see anything.

"Uh..." she whispered, a little worried, "there isn't a chance that's just an enormously delicious grub?" Kyle said nothing and raised his paw to his nose. She knew what that meant. "Shut up and hang on!"

Kee gripped tightly with all six feet, the feathered hairs on each leg meshing with the hairs on Kyle's snout. She tried to sense which direction the threat was moving but could only smell the light, sweet nectar of a nearby patch of milkweed.

Suddenly Kee felt every muscle on Kyle tense, even the ones on his face and snout. Kee tensed too, ready for the bolt. "Here we go," she said to herself, gripping a little harder. She held tightly, waiting for several seconds...but then nothing. *Why aren't we moving?* A light rustling now came from her right. It was getting closer. "What *is* it, Kyle?" She could feel his pulse start to race. *It's circling us*, she thought, starting to panic. *Run Kyle...run!* Another leaf crinkled even closer. *It's practically on top of us now! Do something!*

Just then, Kyle did do something, lunging suddenly and with great force—toward the sound!

"Aaaaagh!" Kee said, barely able to hang on. "What are you—" but before she could finish, he stopped as abruptly as he'd started, throwing her off his head and onto—well, onto something—something moving!

She still couldn't see much, but knew whatever this thing was, it was now fighting...with *Kyle!* She lifted her abdomen and positioned her stinger, ready to plunge, but just then the creature contorted and flipped, almost throwing her off. "Hang on, hang on!" she yelled to herself, trying to regain her footing. *What kind of skin is this?* She felt around frantically with her feet and antennae. *I don't think my stinger will even go through this...and where is its fur?*

Kee was slipping now as she tried to get a good position to plant her stinger. *I've got this. I've got this!* Suddenly the beast flung itself backward, launching Kee into the air and onto Kyle's back. Kyle tumbled backward, almost crushing Kee as she scrambled onto his tail. Then she smelled it. *Musk. Musk! I smell musk! Was I right? Is it a giant grub?*

A streak of moonlight now cut through the dense trees, and she could finally see it…writhing in Kyle's mouth. *That's no grub!*

A long, slithery body wound its way through his mouth and around his back. "Where are its legs?" she yelled to herself, still not quite understanding. The creature was now wrapped around Kyle's neck and starting to squeeze.

The dynamics were changing. She could suddenly feel and smell it. Kyle was struggling. "Oh, no you don't!" Kee yelled, scrambling up Kyle's back toward the writhing mass. *I don't know if I can get my stinger into that weird skin…but if I can get to the eyes*, she thought, climbing over the beast and onto the top of Kyle's head. *Where are you, where are you?* She scanned below, looking for something that looked

like eyes. *There you are!* She noticed a head sticking out of the side of Kyle's mouth.

The beast squeezed again, and Kyle gasped. Kee raced down the front of Kyle's head and then down his snout, suddenly catching Kyle's attention. His eyes tracked her. Even as he struggled for breath, he was now focused on her, worried she was getting too close. As she ran down his nose, his expression started to change from pain...to confusion...and then anger.

What are you doing? Get away from there! he wanted to yell. She continued and then, without hesitation, launched herself from the tip of his nose toward the head of the beast.

From that moment, the next few seconds for Kyle seemed to pass in slow motion...Kee, hanging in air as she slowly descended from his nose toward the flailing head of the beast below. As she glided downward, her body started to re-orient itself, falling abdomen first, her stinger leading the way. *Nooooo!* Kyle thought.

Kee was laser-focused, every one of her almost fourteen thousand lenses bearing straight down on the head of the beast, looking for its vulnerable pupils. That was when she

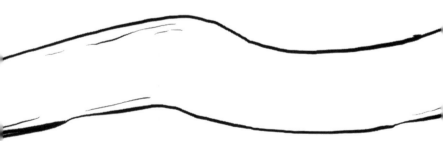

realized a slight miscalculation. This was not the head of the beast at all, but the tail! What she thought were eyes were really markings, designed to do…exactly what they did, distract!

Kyle's own eyes were starting to get blurry now from the lack of oxygen. He had just enough left to give one last chomp, which he did…just as Kee was making contact with the tail of the beast.

The beast flinched, Kyle's mouth fell open, and the three of them dropped to the ground. The beast, seeing its opportunity, released Kyle's neck to escape, then turned to see what had stung him.

Kyle, semiconscious, was lying on the ground, saliva pouring out the side of his mouth. His chest was heaving up and down as he tried to regain his breath. The beast, free from the threat of being eaten, now focused on his own chance for a bite—though a small one.

Kee, worried about Kyle, didn't even notice that the business end of this rubber boa had turned and was now bearing down on her. "Kyle?" she yelled. The snake slid ever so slowly and stealthily so as not to alert his soon-to-be snack.

CHAPTER 5

GOO BALL COMETH

K yle, still groggy and a bit light-headed, lay on his side, snout on the ground in a puddle of his own saliva. His breaths were just starting to calm as he slowly opened his eyes. At first, everything was blurry. He couldn't see anything but could hear something nearby. Then, as his sense of smell returned, *Wait, I know that smell*, he thought, snapping out of it...*snake!*

His head popped up off the ground, but he could still barely see anything. *What is that sound...that crunching? Kee!* He could just make out some movement near his head. He tried to focus and could now see the culprit, its head sliding over a bed of leaves just behind her.

"Kyle?" said a frightened voice.

The beast, now inches from Kee, started to unhinge its jaw and open wide. "Ssssssnack time," it hissed.

Suddenly, a furry black paw crashed down on the beast, causing a big, hairy ball of goo to shoot out of its mouth. "Noodles!" The ball of goo hit Kee, knocking her over. For a few moments, no one moved or said a word. Kee, Kyle, and the snake all just sat and stared…eyes quickly shifting from the goo ball back to each other.

"Uh, what…" Kyle started to speak. "What was that?" His head turned from snake to the now wet pile of fur and back to the snake.

For some reason the "beast" now looked much less menacing, almost shameful. Kyle turned to the creature. "Did you yell something?" he asked, staring directly at the snake. "Noodles?" The snake's eyes just darted around, trying not to make contact, almost pretending like nothing happened.

Kyle turned to Kee with the same inquisitive look, but she just shook her head and pointed to the ball of goo, which was now… "It's moving!" Kee yelled, running to join Kyle. Kee and Kyle stared in amazement as it started to unball itself and transform. It was like they were watching the hatching of an alien egg, unsure what was going to emerge.

Kyle glanced over to the snake, who now gave a very sheepish smile and what almost seemed like a shrug. Kyle turned back toward the grayish ball of fur that was starting to take shape as it shook and wiped itself off.

"It's…it's—" Kee started to say, trying to identify it, but then Kyle finished for her in a perplexed voice: "—a mouse!"

"It's a mouse!" Kee confirmed. "You just saved a mouse's life," she said with pride, patting Kyle's paw with her wing. The snake rolled its eyes.

"Uh, not exactly," said a deep, gravelly voice, startling Kee and Kyle. It continued to brush itself off then shook off the goo and started to wander toward Kee and Kyle. Kee quickly backed up, almost tripping over her own feet, and jumped onto Kyle's paw. The mouse then held out a tiny paw to Kee. "Hi, I'm Pinky." Kee turned and looked to Kyle for some kind of support or assurance. Kyle shrugged at first but then gave her a nod. Kee slowly reached out one antenna to sniff him, but Pinky immediately grabbed it and started shaking. "Nice to meet you," he grumbled, shaking vigorously. "And this slithery rope of flesh over here," he continued, motioning to the snake, "is Noodles…or at least that's what I call him."

"Noodles?" Kyle asked, trying to figure out what was going on. "So you are the one who yelled 'Noodles'?"

Pinky laughed. "Well, it certainly wasn't the snake. Have you ever heard a snake talk?"

Kee and Kyle looked at each other in disbelief, mouths agape. "Am I dreaming this, or did I actually die back there?" Kyle said, putting a paw up to his own neck to check for a pulse. Kee shrugged, confused and now a bit annoyed by this brash ball of fur.

Pinky continued, "And you are?" still shaking her antenna.

"I'm Kee!" she said abruptly, yanking her antenna back out of his paw.

"And your pungent sidekick here?" Pinky said, gesturing toward Kyle with his eyebrows.

"Hey!" Kee snapped. "He's not...he doesn't..." she started to defend but then caught herself, not wanting to hurt Kyle's feelings or give away his secret. "Try a little respect when you meet someone instead of just barging over, hurling insults, grabbing antennas, and...and..." Kyle, sensing she was losing control, gently picked her up in midrant and set her on his nose, where she could settle down. "Hey!" she yelled at Kyle, "I was not finished with him."

"Hi, I'm Kyle." He held his now free paw out to shake Pinky's tiny hand. "We're just a bit on edge right now, what with the recent attempted bee-munching and skunk-strangling and all." They all turned to look at Noodles, who responded with a smirk.

"Wait, wait, wait," Kyle said, still confused by this unsettling pair. "You're together? What...why....how..."

"Don't forget who and when," Pinky mumbled.

"I don't even know where to start! You, you are a mouse...and he...he—"

"Noodles?" Kee interrupted, waving Kyle off with her wing. "Really? You named it?"

"Well, you named yours," Pinky quickly countered. Kee's mouth dropped in shock. Not sure whether she was more offended or outraged, she ran to the tip of Kyle's nose to confront Pinky. Realizing she was not quite close enough, she signaled to Kyle to lower her to get directly in Pinky's face.

"Listen here, you gooey ball of fur," she yelled, waving her wing in Pinky's face from the edge of Kyle's paw.

"You have no right! Who do you think you are with your finger-pointing, antenna-grabbing…and don't get me started on being shot out of…of some slimy, slithery, scaly— " Aware that Kee was at the beginning of another rant, Pinky and Kyle just stared at each other and let her go for a while.

"…who is literally a snake in the grass!" she continued. "If I have to come over there and personally take that tail and—"

"Look, look," Pinky finally interrupted, "I know this is confusing." Kee glared, trying to catch her breath. "I'm a mouse. He's a snake. I just popped out of his mouth. Up is down. Down is up. The world seems a bit topsy-turvy right now. I get it. Here's the deal." He paused, looking at Kee. "You're young, right?"

What does that have to do with anything? she thought, maintaining the glare.

"Life is quite unpredictable," he continued. "Often you expect one thing and then get something altogether different. Or as I like to put it, sometimes life gives you snake." Noodles rolled his eyes. "No offense," Pinky added, glancing at Noodles.

Pinky turned and looked up at Kyle. "You were looking for grub, right?" Kyle nodded, a bit impressed.

"How did he know that?" Kee whispered.

"It's the smell," Pinky said.

"Musk!" all three exclaimed at once. Noodles flicked his tongue a few times to check his own scent.

"You were looking for grub but got snake," Pinky continued. "For me, it was pasta. I was looking for pasta."

Kyle and Kee stared blankly. "You know, pasta, a specific shape of pasta…" He paused again, sure one of them would get it. More blank stares. "Oh come on!" Pinky blurted, getting more frustrated now. "A long pasta…it looks like a snake…starts with 'nnnnnnn'…"

"Mmmmmmm," Kee mimicked.

"No, no, not 'mmmmm,' 'nnnnnnn,'" Pinky said, displaying a wide, toothy grin. Kyle continued to stare blankly, mouth hanging open a bit.

"NOODLES!" Pinky yelled, exasperated. "I named him Noodles because of the pasta!"

"I don't get it," said Kee.

"Seriously? Am I the only one, once again, who has ever heard of pasta?" Pinky scanned for any sign of recognition. Nothing. "So then I guess it is safe to assume," he started, showing off, "that I'm also the only one here who has ever seen…a Baldi?"

CHAPTER 6

THE PACT

A Baldi?" Kee asked, listening intently now. "What is a *Baldi?*" Though she had never personally seen a Baldi, she had heard the stories from others in the hive.

"Baldis are a myth," Kyle whispered. "Don't pay attention." Kee, ignoring Kyle, lay down on his nose, her chin resting on her two front legs so she could focus on Pinky's every word.

"What is a Baldi?" Pinky said, staring at Kee to sense if she was joking. *Hmm, interesting.* "Baldis are only the biggest, baddest, baldest, four-legged—"

"Yeah, yeah, we got it, big, bad, bald," Kyle interrupted. "Can we get back to why you and a snake..."

"Oh, right, right. Long story short," Pinky showed off again, "Baldis like to eat something called 'pasta.' Especially the long, noodley kind." Kee was mesmerized. "Since he looks like a big noodle—"

"Have you seen them? Did you watch them eat? Did they try to eat you?" she interrupted again, pelting Pinky with questions, but Kyle waved her off.

"But why...how...the 'life gives you snake?'" Kyle pressed.

"Right, right," Pinky said. "It was just one of those freak things you never expect. One of those things you think will be terrible...horrible, but then turns out—" He turned to Noodles "—turns out okay. Right, Noods?" Noodles grinned ever so slightly but still rolled his eyes.

"So, go on," Kyle nudged.

"Right. Pretty simple really. He—" Pinky paused, looking a little embarrassed "—ate me. Swallowed me whole...gulp." He made an exaggerated swallowing gesture. Kee's eyes widened in disbelief. "Well, I was quite a bit smaller back then. Just a little guy!" he emphasized. Noodles nodded vigorously in agreement. "And I was all pink, with very little fur."

"Like a Baldi?" Kee said.

Pinky thought for a second. "Yeah, kind of like a Baldi, except for this beautiful tail!" he bragged, swinging his tail around like a sword. "Yes, I am embarrassed to say that as babies we mice look a lot like ugly Baldis!" he said, scrunching up his face.

Kee giggled. "Are they dangerous?" she asked.

"What, the Baldis?"

"Stop interrupting." Kyle stepped in, nudging Kee with a paw. "So, he eats you," he pressed, "go on."

"Right, down I go," Pinky continued, causing Noodles to lick his lips. "Hey, stop that." Kee and Kyle giggled. "For most mice, that would have been the end of the story. But not for—"

"Yeah, yeah, not for you," Kee interrupted yet again. "You're 'Super Mouse'! What about the Baldis?" Kyle picked up a flailing Kee and put her on the end of his tail, gesturing for Pinky to continue. "Hey, that's not fair!" she yelled, already running back toward his head.

"Turns out," Pinky continued, "Smiley over here cannot digest mice. For some reason, his system just can't handle it."

"What?" Kyle asked.

"Yep, Noodles is what you might call 'mouse intolerant.'"

"You've got to be kidding me," Kee said in disbelief.

"Hey, I don't like bees!" Kyle exclaimed, suddenly feeling a connection. "Well, I can tolerate them…" he added, glaring at Kee.

"Thanks a lot," she smirked.

"Most mice," Pinky continued, "just have cardiac arrest before they even get down. Noods likes to kill 'em with kindness, so to speak—he gives 'em a big hug." Pinky demonstrated by hugging himself with both arms. "But with me, he thought I was already dead, so he just swallowed. Actually, I am just a very deep sleeper," he smiled. "So in I went—sound asleep! By the time I woke up, I was already halfway down." Now even Kee was interested, briefly forgetting about the Baldis. "I thought I'd fallen down a hole or something…a very gooey and suspiciously warm hole." Noodles shook his head with a look of disgust. "It wasn't 'til I crawled back up and peeked out his mouth that I realized, 'Cool, I am in a snake!'"

"Cool?" Kee said. "Really?"

"Yeah, I know it sounds weird, but other than the goo and such, I thought it was kind of fun in there. Wasn't much I could do about it anyway, right...or so I thought at the time. If this is how I go, this is how I go. Why give myself added grief and anguish along the way. So I just enjoyed the ride and looked around."

"An explorer!" Kee exclaimed.

"Yeah right, an explorer—seeing, enjoying, and discovering what I can while I can."

"I like that!" Kee said.

Now Kyle shook his head in disbelief. "So you live inside—" He gestured toward Noodles with his head, not wanting to say his name.

"Yes, I live inside—" Pinky giggled and used the same head gesture. "He's kind of my secret fort."

"But how do you eat?" Kee asked. "How does *he* eat?"

"Speaking of eating..." Kyle said, rubbing his belly.

"Lucky for me," Pinky continued, ignoring Kyle, "Noodles and I have some of the same tastes. I like grub, and Noodles puts up with grub." Another eye roll from Noodles. "He just catches a little extra and I...assist him with a little prechewing." Kee gagged and Kyle wrinkled his face in disgust. "Or sometimes *I* go out and do the catching..." Noodles stared at Pinky and shook his head in disagreement. "I go out sometimes!" More eye rolling from Noodles. "I find a grub, chew it up really well, then—"

"Speaking of all this chewing, prechewing, digesting..."

Kyle started, but then his stomach suddenly growled so loudly, it startled Pinky.

"What was that?" He scowled, pinching his nose. "That was disgusting!"

"No, no, that was his stomach!" Kee said. "The other end doesn't work."

"Hey!" Kyle said. Kee grinned awkwardly.

"Well…they did tell us *theirs*," she said. "Seems only fair."

"Yeah, come on, Kyle," Pinky insisted. "We told you ours. Your turn. Share…if you dare!" Kyle rolled his eyes. "Talking about it is the first step," Pinky continued, nudging Kyle with his tail.

"Yeah, like you did to me," Kee added, jumping on the Pinky bandwagon. Kyle glared at Kee.

"We're all friends here," Pinky said. "Well, some formerly known as food, but now friends, right?" Kyle didn't blink. "Ooh, I have an idea," Pinky announced in a loud voice, waking up Noodles. "We will make a pact right now…paws up!" Kee raised two of her three right feet. "Tail up is fine for you," he added, looking at Noodles. "Repeat after me. We promise…"

"We promise," Kee belted out, alone. Pinky gave Kyle a look then turned to Noodles, who started moving his mouth as if repeating the words.

He started again. "We promise…"

"We promise," Kee belted, Kyle mumbled, and Noodles mouthed.

"Not to laugh at others'—" He paused, trying to think of the least offensive word possible "—others' issues…"

"Not to laugh at others' issues," they all continued.

"...except maybe a little at first..."

They all giggled. "...except maybe a little at first..."

"And—" He paused, gathering his thoughts.

"And—"

"And will neither consume nor masticate..."

"What is 'masti...'?" Kee whispered to Kyle.

"To chew."

"Ooh, I like that one!" she said. "And will not consume nor mastri...masticate," she repeated with help from Kyle.

"...those pact members who—" Pinky looked at Noodles, then Kyle "—happen to be riding upon or within us."

"Those who are...on or inside us," Kee and Kyle stumbled through.

"Wait, I have one!" Kee said. She raised her right feet again, gesturing for the others to do the same. The boys looked at each other and then reluctantly complied. "And—" She waited for the response and then gave them all a look and head gesture.

"And—"

"And will support those *upon* and *within* whom we ride," she said with pride. "And the entire group as a whole."

Kyle, Pinky, and Noodles grinned at each other. "And the entire group as a whole."

"Like we are—" She paused, getting a somber and far-away look on her face "—family."

"Fine, fine," Kyle said. "Can we eat now?"

"Yes," Pinky said. "As soon as you share."

Kyle sighed. He'd hoped they had forgotten all about it. Pinky waited in anticipation. Kee gave Kyle a nod of encouragement as she patted his snout with her wing. He looked around at the three pairs of strange but supportive eyes staring at him and finally gave in.

"I," he started, the words getting slightly caught at the back of his throat, "I don't stink. I can't. I…I just don't. I don't know how," he stumbled through. "I…I don't know why, I just don't. I am a skunk…and I don't stink. I am a skunk and I don't stink," he repeated faster and more confidently now. Pinky and Noodles were listening intently, nodding in agreement and understanding, both having experienced their own moments of self-discovery. Kee was watching with pride—and even getting a little teary.

"I am a skunk," he said with power and pride, "and I don't stink. Hello, my name is Kyle, and I don't stink." He giggled. They all laughed, Kee through glassy eyes. Pinky turned and pretended to be coughing so no one could see his tears. Noodles slid his tail around Pinky and slowly pulled him in toward Kyle and Kee. "And I don't care who knows it!" Kyle yelled as they all leaned in for a group hug. "But for now," Kyle whispered, turning to each one of his new friends, "this is just between us, right?" They all chuckled.

"Right!"

"Feels good, doesn't it?" Kee said.

A big smile came over Kyle's face. "Yeah…yes it does. Thank you," he said, looking at each one of them—except for Pinky, who was looking the other way.

Kee nudged him. "Pinky, you okay there?" she said with a grin.

"Yeah, yeah," he said through the obvious sniffles. "Allergies."

Kee smiled. "I'm allergic to bees!" They all laughed.

"Can we eat now?" Kyle said.

"Yes, quickly, before he goes back on his pact," Pinky said.

"I don't suppose you have any extra grub lyin' around in that 'secret fort'—" Kyle made air quotes with his paws "—of yours, would ya?" Pinky grinned one of those guilty kind of grins, and Noodles just shook his head.

Pinky got a big smile. "Grub run?"

"Grub run!" Kyle said. Noodles licked his lips.

"And if we just happen to see a flower along the way, a nectar run?" Kee said.

"Let's go!" Kyle said.

"Woo-hoo!" Kee yelled. "We have a posse!"

Noodles opened his jaws wide. Pinky jumped in and turned for a last wave before yelling, "To the grub!" Noodles' jaw slowly closed and then, with a gulp, a Pinky-sized bulge started to make its way down.

"That's just not right," Kyle said, staring in disbelief.

"That was cool!" Kee said.

"A-grubbin' we will go. A-grubbin' we will go," Kee started, with Kyle joining in, "Hi-ho the derry-o, a-grubbin' we will go."

Noodles opened his mouth, and from deep within, a gruff and muffled voice could be heard. "A-grubbin' we will go!"

Kee jumped with delight.

CHAPTER 7

RUMBLER TRACKS

And a-grubbin' they went. For the rest of the night, Kyle and Noodles walked and slithered over hills, through woods, and across fields. The two of them, both "night owls," so to speak, were now in their element. Noodles loved the cool and calm that darkness brings, while Kyle loved the opportunity to fill his tummy. Many of the delicacies they would usually pursue sleep at night…including their two passengers!

Kee tried to stay awake for the first hour or so, helping to guide Kyle to any nearby field of clover or daisy. "No, to the right. I smell it more to the right," she whispered from the edge of his ear, not wanting to alert other predators.

Pinky, on the other hand, not used to having a band of traveling companions, kept peeking his head out of Noodles' mouth (just to say hi, he said). The real reason, of course, was that he was already missing his new compadres and wanted to make sure they were still there. "To the left…no left. They're over there!" Pinky grumbled, suddenly emerging from Noodles' mouth. He would stand in Noodles' jaws like he was holding open a garage door, both hands over his head, straining against the top jaw, all the while barking out navigational instructions. "Faster! Come on, we're losing them!"

"Slow down," Kee said, pulling back on Kyle's right ear like it was horse reins.

Needless to say, these barking copilots did not hold their positions long—for two reasons. The first: neither Kyle nor Noodles particularly appreciated the art of backseat driving. When Kyle had enough, he would just pick Kee up off his ear and set her back on the very tip of his tail. That usually gave him two or three minutes of whisper-free travel time—which includes the minute of pouting time before she would scramble up the tail and back onto his ear.

Noodles had a quicker and easier solution. He would simply slam his mouth shut and swallow. Well, it wasn't exactly a slam. Pinky always fought it at first—his little arms and legs trembling at the knees and elbows, straining to hold the "door" open—until he could hold it no longer, yelling as the jaw slammed closed. "Nood—!" is all that could be heard, the last syllable muffled by the acoustical damping of a southbound mouse in a northbound snake.

The second reason these little drivers did not drive long was exhaustion. All the excitement and activity of the day had left both Pinky and Kee dog-tired, so to speak. On top of that, unlike Kyle and Noodles, night time was their sleep time.

Before long, Kee was sound asleep, snuggled up in Kyle's right ear. He thought about moving her to his snout—Kee was a snorer—but soon got used to the light rumblings in his ear…and even liked it. Occasionally he could even hear her dreaming. "Baldi ate my lunch!" she mumbled from a stupor, then more snoring. "My hive. My hive!" She rustled a bit, then back to snoring. "Grub 'n noodles, grub 'n noodles, grub 'n noodles…"

Fortunately for Noodles, his passenger was, as advertised, a very heavy sleeper. No snoring. No dreams. No tossing. Pinky slept so quietly and still, in fact, that Noodles would occasionally regurgitate him just to make sure he was okay. Out he would come, *plop*, a big, damp hairball falling out of Noodles' mouth onto the ground, sound asleep. Then back in he went, still asleep. Every morning, right on schedule, Pinky would stir, stretch, and then wander up and down his gooey abode to see what Noodles might have swallowed that night.

But that is not how Pinky awakened *that* morning. It was just about dawn, still quite dark, but a slight lightening could now be seen in the eastern sky. Kyle and Noodles had already collected quite a few grubs when Kyle noticed a patch of flowers across the way. Excited to surprise Kee with a tasty breakfast, he dashed toward the field…when he suddenly heard, "Kyle!"

Pinky sensed a type of vibration and alarm within Noodles he had not felt before. Kyle came to a sudden stop, so abruptly that Kee almost fell off his head. Kyle's breathing was fast and heavy, his heart beating three times its normal rate. Noodles was about ten feet away at the edge, his heart and respiration also racing. Kyle and Noodles stared at each other with the same look of fear and confusion.

Kee, jarred from her sleep, groggily climbed back up the side of Kyle's head and onto his snout. "What are you trying to do—" she started to say, but then saw the look of fear in Kyle's eyes. "What? What's wrong? What happened?" She spun around to see Pinky emerging from Noodles' mouth.

Pinky, still a bit groggy, suddenly snapped out of it when he saw Kyle. "Rumbler tracks," he mumbled, stepping down onto the ground. Noodles immediately corralled Pinky back in with his tail. Then Kee saw it. The ground Kyle was standing on wasn't like anything she had seen before. It was smooth, dark, and cold—strangely absent of grass, trees, bushes, or any living thing…except for the two of them.

"What—" Kee stammered. "What is this, Kyle?" He didn't respond, staring blankly toward Noodles. Kee turned and looked him directly in the eye. "Kyle…Kyle? What is this? Where are we?"

Although he had heard all about the dangers of Rumblers, how fast they were and almost always deadly, he had never actually seen one. But now here he was in the dead center of a well-used set of Rumbler tracks.

"Kyle!" Kee said again, waving her wing frantically. Kyle, frozen in fear, didn't respond.

Pinky yelled now from the side of the tracks. "Kyle, listen to me," he instructed calmly but sternly. "Walk back toward me. One step at a time. Right, then left." Kyle, still breathing heavily, turned his head and looked at Pinky but couldn't move.

"It's okay, Kyle," Kee tried to reassure, still a bit confused by the urgency of the situation. "You can do this. Just take your time."

"Here we go," Pinky encouraged. "Left, right, left, right..." He mimicked, marching his feet up and down.

Kyle looked down at his own feet, then back to Pinky with an expression of frightened frustration. Nothing was moving. "You've got this, Kyle," Pinky continued. "Like Kee said, just take your ti—" Pinky stopped in midsentence as something flashed, momentarily blinding him. Pinky rubbed his eyes and turned to his right to see the unmistakable piercing eyes of a Night Rumbler.

"What...what is that?" Kee said.

"Kyle!" Pinky said with a new intensity. "You have to move, Kyle! Think, Kyle. You must move your legs!"

Kee stood at the bottom of Kyle's right eye, staring into his pupil, her front legs stretched up onto his open eye lid. "Kyle...Kyle?...KYLE!" She now spoke with the same stern and deliberate force as Pinky. "Look at me, Kyle. You... can...do this!" His fear momentarily distracted by this bug in his eye, he finally looked at Kee—and then saw the Rumbler closing in behind her.

"Come on, Kyle!" Pinky yelled.

With tears of frustration streaming down Kyle's face, his legs refusing to move, he summoned one last bit of will and focus, brought his right paw up to his nose, and flung Kee toward Pinky.

"Noooo!" she screamed, flying through the air.

Noodles quickly slithered onto the tracks toward the falling Kee. The Rumbler was bearing down on Kyle, getting closer and closer. Then, from out of nowhere, a gust of wind caught Kee, blowing her back toward Kyle.

"Noooo!" he yelled, still unable to move his feet. The Rumbler was dangerously close now as Kee floated back to Kyle.

Pinky pulled on Noodles' tail to get him back off the tracks. The Rumbler was almost on top of Kyle. He looked at the Rumbler, turned to Pinky and Noodles, then took a last look at Kee, who was now back within reach. There was a sharp pain, a jolting blindness, and then nothing.

CHAPTER 8

LOST

Morning sunlight was just starting to peek through the trees as Pinky and Noodles sat next to Kyle on the side of the road. Pinky sat on Kyle's chest while Noodles surrounded and held them both.

"Kyle?" Pinky said, poking him in the snout with a paw. No response. "Come on, buddy, wake up," he tried again, scrambling up his snout and lifting an eyelid. "I know you're in there."

"Squeeze him again," Pinky barked. Kyle's face bulged as Noodles' coils tightened around him. "Easy, we don't want to pop an eye out. One more time."

Kyle's face swelled once again, then suddenly gasped. "Kee!" he said, eyes snapping open.

"There you are!" Pinky said, a big smile on his face. "You made it!"

"Where's Kee?"

"Whoa, slow down, big guy. You have been through quite an ordeal."

"Where is she?" Kyle tried getting up but then stumbled, disoriented.

"Stop," Pinky said. "You're hurt!"

Kyle ignored him, scanning the surrounding area for any sign of her. "Where is Kee?"

Pinky nervously looked over at Noodles, then back to Kyle. "We…don't know," Pinky said, sounding worried.

"What do you mean you don't know? Where is she?" Kyle said, putting a paw up to his right eye, now throbbing and swollen closed.

"Honestly, we don't know—" Pinky looked at Noodles for support "—for sure."

"What does that mean? Kee!" Kyle yelled, taking a step, but then stumbling in pain.

"I think it's just a sprain." Pinky pointed at a puffy area just above Kyle's left hind paw. Kyle glared at Noodles and Pinky.

"We looked! We looked all around but couldn't find her."

Kyle stared in frustration. "What happened?" he finally asked, taking some time to compose himself. "Just tell me what you know. I remember—" He paused, trying to piece things together "—I remember a Rumbler. It was closing in on us. Kee was…she was…I threw her!" he said, his memory starting to return. "I threw Kee! I threw her—" His face suddenly changed from a look of confusion to anger "—to *you*! I remember now. Did you *not* catch her?

Did you? What did you do?" he yelled, losing control. He tried to stand but stumbled again.

"Stop!" Pinky begged. Noodles put his tail around Kyle, trying to soothe, but was shoved away.

"What did you do?"

"Nothing. Nothing, I swear! The wind caught her and she blew back to you."

Kyle thought for a moment. His face strained, trying to recall the last few moments before blackout. "Yes, yes…right. You're right. She was coming back to me…" He struggled to picture what happened next. "Then…" His expression suddenly changed from concern to dread. "Was it me? Did I…did I not catch her? I…I can't remember." He was getting frustrated with himself. "Please help me. Please, please!" Pinky looked at Noodles, not sure how much to divulge. "Please tell me what happened."

"Okay." Pinky sighed. Kyle stared intently, not sure whether he really wanted to know what he was about to hear. Pinky took a deep breath. "I will tell you, but it's not much." Kyle nodded, eyes locked on Pinky. "Here is all we know." Pinky looked at Noodles once again for support. "The Rumbler was bearing down…you flung Kee toward us to get her out of harm's way, one of the most selfless, bravest—"

"Yeah, yeah," Kyle interrupted. "Then what?"

"It was the wind. A gust suddenly came up and swept her back to you…and…"

"And…and? Then?"

Pinky hesitated, getting a solemn look on his face. "She stung you." Kyle's mouth dropped, and he grabbed his right eye.

"In the eye," Kyle said calmly.

"Yeah."

Tears rolled down Kyle's face as the full impact started to sink in. "She knew that would jolt me—get me to move."

Pinky looked up at a slumped Kyle and put a paw on his foot. Noodles wrapped them both up in his coils, pulling them close. They each stared in silence for a while, trying to take it all in. It had all happened so fast.

Kyle wiped his nose with his paw, took a deep breath, and rubbed both eyes, wincing slightly as he touched the right. "So," he finally asked, breaking the silence, "where is she?"

Pinky and Noodles looked at each other, a little confused at first by the question. "Um...I don't know," Pinky said, struggling to understand the point.

"Let's find her."

For a moment, Pinky didn't know what to say, a very uncommon occurrence for him. The thought of a search seemed at best depressing, and at worst—well, he didn't want to think about it. He briefly considered discouraging Kyle from this idea but was quickly dissuaded by the look of resolve on Kyle's face. He wanted to see her one last time. He needed to say goodbye.

"We *did* look around," Pinky said, concerned by the additional pain and anguish this could cause. "It is possible that her body is..." Pinky hesitated, not wanting to give Kyle any crazy ideas.

"...on the Rumbler." Kyle completed the sentence. Pinky nodded.

"It could be anywhere," Pinky said. "And worse—"

"Baldis." Kyle again finished the thought.

"Yes, Baldis."

"Well," Kyle said, looking more determined than ever, "good thing we have a Baldi expert on our team then."

Kyle got up and started limping down the side of the road. Pinky looked at Noodles, who looked back with the same expression—*this is really a bad idea.* "I don't suppose we can talk you out of this, can we?" Pinky yelled at Kyle's back as he continued down the road.

"Come on," Pinky moaned. "I guess we better—" He turned to Noodles, only to discover he was already gone. "Good job, Pinky," he mumbled to himself. "You had to make a pact."

CHAPTER 9

THE LEGEND OF LUCKY

S low down!" Pinky said, already winded. "Come on, Noodles! You never move this fast when I'm along for the…oh, right." Kyle and Noodles were side by side now, with Pinky trailing far behind. "You know, Kyle," Pinky bellowed, holding his side, "this really isn't good for your ankle!"

Kyle, noticing Noodles beside him, looked over and smiled. "So you left the little runt behind, huh?" Noodles grinned and kept slithering.

"Come on guys…really?" Pinky said, falling even farther behind. He stopped for a second to catch his breath. "I really need to get outside a little more," he grumbled to himself.

Kyle looked over his shoulder to a small puff of dust trailing in the distance and felt a little guilty. "Do you think we should slow down?" Noodles put his head down and accelerated. "I'll take that as a 'No.'" He took a few more steps. "Come on. We can let him catch up. Don't you think we've tortured him enough? Besides, my ankle could use a rest." Noodles stopped, to Pinky's delight.

"Thanks, guys," he yelled, giving them a wave. "Thanks for waiting!" Kyle and Noodles watched as Pinky slowly whined and moaned his way toward them. "If you are trying to kill me," he gasped, almost up to the guys, "just eat me and be done with it!" Kyle and Noodles turned to each other and grinned.

"Oh...one more thing before he gets here," Kyle whispered, watching Pinky inch closer, "I know your little secret." Noodles turned and stared at the side of Kyle's head. "Don't worry...it's safe with me." Noodles looked both surprised and confused.

"Hey, Pinky." Kyle greeted their tired friend. "What took you so long?"

Pinky wheezed, rolled over onto his back, and stuck all four legs straight up. "Aaagh!" Kyle and Noodles both snickered.

"So, Mr. Baldi-mouse," Kyle asked, "what's the plan?"

"What?" Pinky panted, still trying to catch his breath. "Are you talkin' to me? This was *your* idea!"

"True," Kyle said, "but you are clearly the only one with true Baldi experience. We haven't seen or dealt with them like you have." Kyle gestured to himself and Noodles.

Pinky slowly rolled onto his side and gave Kyle a look of disbelief. "Hold on...wait a minute. I thought you didn't even believe in Baldis." Kyle glanced away with a slight look of guilt. "That's right, I heard you tell Kee they were only a myth."

"Yes, I did say that…but only to protect her. Besides, it isn't really the Baldis that I think are a myth. It is a *specific* Baldi."

"Ooh, let me guess…" Pinky jumped in, pretending to think about it. "Hmm…who could it be? Would you happen to be referring to… perhaps… the legend of Lucky?"

"Yeah, that's the one," Kyle acknowledged, a bit deflated.

"But everyone knows that one—" Pinky looked at the two of them, a little disappointed "—right?" Noodles nudged Pinky in the side with his tail. "What? Seriously? You've never heard of Lucky?" Noodles stared blankly. "Well—" Pinky turned to Kyle "—will you tell him or shall I?"

"The story goes like this…" Kyle started.

"No, wait! Why are you telling it?" Pinky interrupted. "You don't even think it's real."

"It's not!"

"Don't listen to him," Pinky mumbled.

"Go ahead then, you tell it," Kyle said.

"No, I'm too tired. You do it."

Kyle glanced at Noodles with a look of bewilderment, like one parent blaming the other for the hooligan in their midst. Noodles grinned.

Kyle started again. "So, as the legend goes, there is this mythical being—"

"Actual," Pinky blurted. "He is real!"

"Am I telling this or you?" Kyle said. Pinky put a paw over his own mouth and gestured to proceed. "The legend goes that there is a creature—"

"Baldi."

Noodles, tired of the interruptions, suddenly opened his jaws wide and dropped them over Pinky's head like an oversized snake hat.

"Well, that should do it," Kyle said. Noodles signaled with his tail to continue.

"So this creature, a Baldi, is not like—"

"Could you speak up, please!" A muffled request came from deep within Noodles' mouth.

"This particular Baldi," Kyle continued, "known as 'Lucky,' is supposed to have the ability to make anyone feel better. The sick, the poor, the troubled—heck, even the mildly disgruntled—all tell of visiting this magic, voodoo…"

"Not voodoo. Not voodoo!" A comment came from within Noodles.

"…all by visiting or just being near this creature," Kyle continued. "This is why I told Kee that Baldis are a myth. I didn't want her to get her hopes up. I think she wanted to find this Lucky character…to get her wing—"

"Enough!" Pinky belted, throwing open Noodles' mouth with both hands over his head. "Your turn, my stinky friend, is ove—" Pinky dropped one hand to point at Kyle, and Noodles' mouth slammed shut over his head again. "Noodles!" came a distant plea. Noodles' eyes gleamed. His jaw slowly raised again, revealing Pinky, annoyed and breathing quite heavily in an overhead press. "Do–you–mind?" Pinky grumbled. "Just hold it open!" The corners of Noodles' mouth raised to a sly grin. "Snakes!" Pinky mumbled.

"Enough of this fairytale mumbo jumbo! Lucky is not

magic, does not use voodoo…and most definitely is not a myth!" said Pinky. Noodles looked skeptical. Kyle rolled his eyes. "I have seen her—him—her…" Pinky stumbled.

"Wait. What?" Kyle said. "Which is it, a he or a she?"

Pinky suddenly felt a bit muddled. "Well, uh…I'm not sure. It's been awhile."

"What does that mean?"

"Well, he was a 'he'—is a 'he'…I think. But then the one I met was a she…"

"Whoa, whoa, whoa." Kyle stopped him. "The *one* you met? There is more than one?"

Pinky scratched his head and looked around, a little confused. "Yeah…"

"What was that?" Kyle pressed.

"Yes…yes, that's it!" Pinky spoke now with more confidence. "That explains it! I could never figure out that part…" His voice trailed off as he mumbled to himself with excited delight. "First a he, then a she. How was that possible?"

"Pinky!" Kyle yelled. "You're mumbling!"

"Oh, right, right. That's it," he now declared calmly. "There is more than one Lucky!" Kyle and Noodles stared. "And I know just where to find one. She can help us find Kee."

"Let's go!" said Kyle.

CHAPTER 10

SANDY'S DINER

T wo front wheels turned off the pavement and into a gravel parking lot. A cloud of dust billowed from behind, eventually passing all eighteen wheels as they came to a stop. Country music could be heard coming from inside: *I'm a little biscuit on your gravy train...* The engine rumbled to a stop, followed shortly by the music. There was a *clack*, a small bounce, *crunch, crunch*, then *slam*. More crunches as footsteps trailed away. A few seconds later, the *thump, thump* of boots on hardwood, the *creak* of a screen door, then *whap!*

"Welcome to Sandy's," said a springy voice. "Oh, morning, Joe."

"Morning, Sally," responded a deep, sleepy voice. A padded counterside stool squeaked as it rotated out and back. A ceramic coffee cup *clunked* as it was set on the vinyl counter. More country music could be heard coming from the kitchen: *It's not uncouth to brush my tooth…*

"The usual?" Sally asked.

Joe, still sleepy, thought for a moment. "Any lunch specials?" Sally shuffled some sheets of paper then slapped one down on the counter. "Hmm…give me the number one.

"Fried, flamed, or fricasseed?"

"Uh, flamed."

"Chicken Leg #1…on the barbecue," she yelled back to the kitchen. "Anything for your friend there?" Confused, he turned, looking behind. No one. "No, there—on your arm," she added.

"Aaagh!" He flicked something off his sleeve.

"Oh, come on. Why'd ya go and do that?" Sally grumbled, looking around on the floor. "Where did it go?"

Meanwhile, at the far left edge of the parking lot, a stone's throw from the front door, a skunk, snake, and mouse peered nervously through a patch of tall grass at a small structure with an old, rickety sign reading, "andy's – Good Grub." A big "S" dangled sideways just below the "a."

"This is a bad idea," Kyle mumbled.

"No kidding," Pinky said. "I told you that hours ago."

Kyle stared at the sign, licking his lips. "Besides, we don't have time for this. We need to find Kee!"

"True," Pinky said, "but we need energy to do that—haven't rustled up anything in quite a while." Kyle's tummy grumbled loudly, briefly startling both Pinky and Noodles. "Oh, come on!" Pinky winced, pinching his nose.

"It's my stomach!" Kyle said. Pinky's fingers stayed put, just in case.

"Are you sure we want to do thi—" Pinky started, but then froze, suddenly noticing Noodles slithering across the gravel lot toward the side of the building.

"Noodles!" Kyle yelled under his breath. He briefly looked at Pinky, scanned the lot in both directions, and then hobbled after Noodles.

Pinky shook his head in bewilderment. "Snakes!" he grumbled and left his perch in the grass.

The three huddled behind a small but pungent sumac bush just this side of the porch. Kyle and Pinky were breathing heavily, partly from the jaunt, mostly from nerves. Noodles stared calmly, scanning the parking lot and front door.

"This is stupid…this is stupid." Kyle groaned and started to nervously interrogate Pinky about Baldis. "Okay, okay. If I get caught, what do I need to do? Does biting work? Scratching? Clawing? You do remember, I can't stink, right?"

"Calm down!" Pinky snapped, though feeling just as jittery as Kyle. "You're the one who thought we should—" Suddenly Noodles shot out of the bush, onto the wooden deck, and slithered over toward the entrance. Pinky and Kyle's jaws dropped. Noodles slid his head around the edge of the screen door, nudging it open slightly. Kyle and Pinky momentarily sat transfixed in shock. They then turned, gave each other a nod of support, and stepped gingerly onto the porch. Just then, Noodles' tail flipped straight up. They both froze in the middle of the porch. Kyle started shaking. Pinky's tail twitched. For once, they were both thinking the same thing. *We're going to die!* After what seemed like an eternity, Noodles gave another tail signal. *Come!* They both swallowed the lumps in their throats and lightly but quickly scampered to the door.

Suddenly, for the first time, Kyle heard the chaos and hubbub of the Baldi world. A cacophony of chatter, music, and the *clink and clank* of utensils poured out of the door. Panicked, Kyle turned to run back to the bush—just as another Rumbler pulled into the lot. Noodles threw open the door with his tail, corralled his two frozen compadres, and yanked them inside. There was a quick *creak*, then *whap!*

"Welcome to Sandy's, sit anywhere you li—" Sally

stopped short, not seeing anyone there. Leaves rustled on a potted ficus tree next to the door. "Hmm...wind," she mumbled. Noodles had wrapped himself around the bottom of the trunk while Kyle hid behind the pot with Pinky clinging to his tail. Kyle, his heart nearly beating out of his chest, still couldn't see any actual Baldis from this position, but was mesmerized—and terrified—by their sounds and smells.

Noodles was winding himself up the tree trunk to get a better vantage point when a tater tot rolled around the back of a booth and stopped under a "Wet Floor" sign. The three of them froze, waiting to see if someone or something was following. Nothing. Noodles scanned the area and gave Pinky the "all clear." Pinky shook his head, not ready to let go of Kyle's tail. Noodles looked around again, gave him a more forceful signal, and then nudged him off Kyle's tail. Pinky dropped to the floor. He peeked around Kyle's tail then dashed across the walkway to the tot. Unfortunately, the floor was as advertised. Pinky missed the target, sliding well past both sign and tater, and came to a stop under an empty table. Noodles and Kyle both gasped from their respective tree lookouts.

Pinky was shaking, feeling way too exposed. He looked back to the tree, anxious for a signal to return. Noodles checked the surroundings once again and gave him the nod. Pinky launched himself from under the table. Just then, a sound came out of Noodles that Pinky had never heard before: his voice. "Kee!" Pinky put on the brakes, sliding once again past the "Wet Floor" sign and coming to a stop—in the middle of the walkway.

CHAPTER 11

ROGUE DRONE

A chubby, ketchup-laden hand reached for the apple sauce, knocking another tater tot onto the floor, where it rolled behind the booth. "Uh-ohhh," squealed a small voice.

Sally giggled. "No problem, sweetie," she said in her baby voice. "I'll get it." There was a sudden violent shaking of the ficus, then a *slap* of something hitting the linoleum floor. "Huh?" Sally mumbled, turning toward the door. More shuffling, then quiet.

Sally wandered around the edge of the booth to the front walkway. She turned the corner, scanned the area, saw nothing out of the ordinary—just a few extra ficus leaves on the floor—and maybe that "Wet Floor" sign slightly askew. *What's with the wind today?* she thought, heading over to adjust the sign.

Kyle froze, suddenly getting a glimpse of his first Baldi, or at least the hind legs of a Baldi. *No fur. They have no fur! They really are bald!* he thought, staring at two bare legs walking by—legs that were now headed directly toward the sign concealing Noodles and Pinky.

Noodles, in a last-ditch effort, was able to upright the sign Kyle had knocked over while trying to save Pinky. Kyle then scrambled under the table and was now staring at Noodles, stretched horizontally across the bottom of the sign, forcing its sides apart. In the meantime, Pinky had jammed himself up against the top point of the sign and was now locked in a steely-eyed staring contest with a strange bee, just an inch from his nose.

"Who the heck are you?" Pinky angrily whispered, expecting to see Kee. "It's not her!" a disappointed Pinky whispered down to Noodles.

A rugged and extremely confident—albeit one-winged—drone pointed his abdomen in Pinky's direction. "I will gladly use this, my tiny friend," the stranger threatened in a deep and somewhat exotic voice.

"Nice try." Pinky chuckled, knowing male bees have no actual stingers. "Bring it on, Zorro!" he mocked, swishing his tail like a sword.

The drone did not flinch, his intense gaze piercing straight through Pinky. "My name is Rohan," he declared. "I have but one mission, to find and serve my queen."

"Oh, I bet you do," Pinky said snidely. "How's that going for you, big guy? Isn't it true, you only get one shot at—"

"Shhhh!" interrupted Noodles, watching Sally approach.

"Oh, really?" Pinky turned his irritation on Noodles. "After all this time, you finally decide to speak, and all you can give me is 'Shhhh?'"

"SHHHH!" Noodles said, more forcefully this time.

"That's low, man!" Pinky said. Rohan nodded in agreement. Pinky gave him a dirty look.

They all held their breath as a pair of Baldi legs stopped next to the sign. "Don't move!" Pinky whispered slowly to Rohan, who rolled his eyes. Sally bent down and picked up the sign, causing Noodles to briefly loose his grip and dangle out the bottom. Kyle gasped. She carried the sign to the center of the walkway as Noodles reeled his tail back in, then set it down and returned to her station. An audible sigh of relief came from under the table.

"Come on, let's move!" said Noodles, wasting no time.

Pinky waved to Rohan as he started down the sign. "Adios, muchacho."

"Wait!" Rohan said. Pinky kept moving. "If you see my queen—"

"Yeah, yeah," Pinky interrupted, "we will send her your love."

"She has just one wing, so it might be difficult..." Rohan continued. Noodles and Pinky stopped in their tracks, staring at each other.

What's taking them so long? Kyle grumbled to himself from under the table. Confused about Kee, afraid of these strange Baldis, and feeling alone, he started to break down.

Is Kee in there? he thought. *Did they find her? Why did Noodles yell her name? Where is she?* He moaned, starting to feel the full remorse of losing his little friend. *What's happening? Where are you, Kee? I'm sorry...I'm just so sorry...I—I never meant...I never...* He put his head down in his paws, tears rolling down his cheeks. "I miss you," he mumbled aloud now. He sniffled, then started to chuckle, realizing what he was saying. "I miss you. You're a bee with one wing—and I'm a skunk that doesn't stink— and I miss y—" He suddenly felt something on his right front paw. He opened his eyes and looked down.

"I miss you too," Kee said with a smile, staring up at him through equally teary eyes.

"Aaaagh!" Kyle said with delight, scooping her up ever so gently with both paws and setting her on his nose. "You're alive. You're alive! How is this poss—I don't care." He interrupted himself. "You're ALIVE!"

"Shhhh!" she said quietly, hugging his swollen eyelid. "Let's keep it that way."

Kyle nodded with a huge grin then realized the guys didn't know. "Oh my gosh, we have to tell the guys! They're gonna be so excited. And so much to tell you, too! So much has happened since you..."

"Since I stung you?" Kee said.

"So you *did* sting me?" Kee nodded with a slight look of guilt. Kyle smiled. "Right in the eye! Thanks a lot! I can still barely open it."

"You're welcome," she said with a smile.

His expression suddenly changed from joyful to puzzled.

"But how—how are you still here? And how did you get—*here?*"

Inside the "Wet Floor" sign, the boys were having similar revelations. "She's a queen?" Pinky asked, half excited, half in disbelief.

"That means she could still be alive," said Noodles, calm but hopeful.

"Well, look at you with full sentences," Pinky said snidely.

"I certainly hope she's still alive," Rohan said in a serious tone. "We have a couple of very nasty princesses about ready to overthrow her. They think she's abandoned the hive."

"Kee wouldn't do that!" Pinky said.

"If we don't find her soon," Rohan added, "today, in fact, it may be too late. The hive is on the move!"

"She's a queen!" Pinky exclaimed proudly, still trying to convince himself.

"Yes, she is. We just need to find her. And we need to do so before that skunk gets around to—"

Pinky laughed. "Oh no, he's with us."

"But—but…" Rohan started, but Pinky waved him off.

"Don't ask. I live with a snake." He pointed at Noodles. "Kee and the skunk are besties. It's a whole freakshow. Best just leave it alone." Rohan looked confused. "Ooh, that reminds me, Kyle still doesn't know! She is a queen—and could be alive!"

Noodles turned to Rohan. "Where do we look?"

"Well, I smelled her near here," Rohan said. "I think she's close."

"Come on," Noodles said, heading back down the sign. "Let's get Kyle and go find Kee."

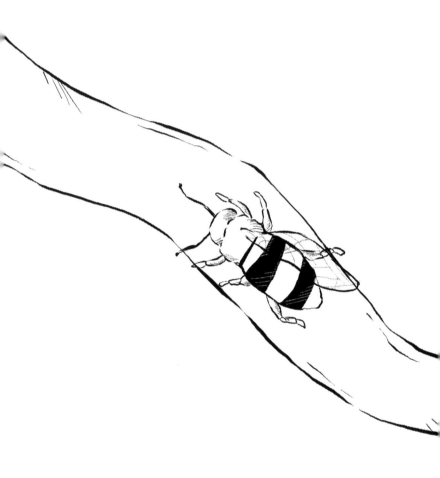

Pinky put his arm around Rohan. "Stick with me, kid. I'll look after ya." Rohan shrugged his arm off his shoulder and followed Noodles.

Noodles peeked out the bottom of the sign, looked around, then gave Pinky and Rohan a signal with his tail.

Move! Noodles shot across the floor, Rohan perched on his back.

"Hey!" Pinky yelled. "That's *my* ride!"

From under the table, Kyle heard the boys stirring. "They're on their way," he whispered to Kee, "let's surprise them," picking her up off his nose and setting her on his tail. Just then, Noodles came around the corner. "Noodles!" Kyle yelled, trying to suppress his joy. "You won't believe who I—" Kyle stopped in midsentence, noticing a strange passenger on Noodles' back. "Who is this?" he asked suspiciously.

"I—I am Rohan," he stuttered, never having actually spoken to a skunk before. "And I will gladly use this, sir," he said once again, bluffing. Kee, hearing a strange voice, scurried up Kyle's back to get a peek. "I have but one mission," Rohan continued in his most official and manly voice, "to find and serve the—" He suddenly froze, seeing Kee poke her head out from behind Kyle's ear. "Your Majesty!" he said, instinctively bowing before her.

Kyle spun around to see who he was talking to, almost throwing Kee off his head. "Who are you—" he started to say, but then noticed Kee climbing down the front of his head. Kee and Rohan locked eyes. "Oh!" He laughed. "No, that is just Kee. She's not a—"

Suddenly Pinky barged in, arriving late on the scene. "Kyle, Kyle!" he interrupted, barreling into the side of Noodles. "Guess what we foun—" But he stopped, noticing Kee and Rohan staring at each other.

"He knows," Noodles said, covering Pinky's mouth with his tail. "He knows."

CHAPTER 12

SNAKE TALK

Kee climbed out onto the end of Kyle's nose to get a better look at Rohan, who bowed. "Oh stop, stop!" Kee said. "No bowing, please. That's just weird." He slowly rose and stood nervously, looking almost straight up at Kee perched atop the towering skunk. "Hi," she said sweetly, waving her one wing with a big smile.

"Good day, Your Majesty." He awkwardly waved his one wing.

"No, please. No 'Your Majestys.'" She scrambled down the side of Kyle's head and lowered herself down his right paw. Rohan ran over to help. She turned around and suddenly found herself face-to-face with him—or nearly so. He being larger than most drones and she smaller than most queens, Kee actually had to look up to make eye contact. "Hi," she gulped, "I'm Kee."

"H—hello," he stuttered, breathing heavily. "I'm…I'm…"

"Rohan," Kyle finished for him. "Your name is Rohan." Rohan nodded.

Noodles and Pinky started to fidget, suddenly feeling a little like third wheels. "Get a honeycomb already," Pinky murmured. Noodles jabbed him with his tail.

"So—" Kyle changed subjects, trying to break the awkwardness "—about this chatterbox over here…" He gestured to a grinning Noodles.

"Yeah, right!" Pinky said. "I even heard him say a full sentence! I believe it was, 'Shhh.'" They all laughed, except Noodles, who once again rolled his eyes.

"So, Noodles, what's up?" Kyle continued. "Why have you been so quiet until now? What's your story?" They all stared, waiting for a response. Noodles grinned.

"Come now, come now," Kee chimed in, momentarily peeling her attention away from Rohan. "I too am fascinated to hear our noble Noodles speak. Kyle was just telling me all about your recent utterings."

Noodles squirmed a bit, scanning the small crowd of eyes all looking in his direction. Kyle grinned. Pinky smirked. Kee nodded and gestured support with her wing. Rohan simply copied Kee.

Noodles gulped. "Are you sure this is the most appropriate time and venue, my lady?" he suddenly said in a warm, deep voice.

"Wee hee!" They all erupted with delight.

"Did you hear that?" said Pinky with a big grin.

"Shhh, shhh!" Kee said, not wanting to push their luck.

Kyle and Pinky giggled. Rohan started to giggle but quickly stopped when Kee looked over.

"Appropriate time and venue..." Pinky mocked, causing more giggles.

"My lady?" Kyle joined in on the light ribbing. "No, I believe she is *my* lady."

"No, *my* lady!" said Pinky.

They all turned to Rohan, who squirmed nervously. Kee reached down with her left wing and touched his right.

The giggling settled down, and Noodles continued. "Rohan had mentioned an imminent deadline?"

"Imminent deadline," Pinky mumbled with a grin. "You're killing me, Noods!"

Kee scanned the immediate area, smelling the surrounding air with her antennae. "We have time, Noodles," she assured him, though Rohan seemed a bit anxious. "Share," she continued. "What happened?"

Noodles gathered his thoughts, looking around at the unlikely band of eyes and ears around him. Pinky sat on his haunches, hands under his chin. Kyle picked up Kee and Rohan and set them atop his nose. All eyes were on Noodles. He glanced at each one: Pinky gave a thumbs-up, Kyle a grin, Rohan remained stoic, and Kee nodded reassuringly.

"Ya want me to warm 'em up for ya?" Pinky offered, starting to get up. They all giggled.

"You've warmed them quite enough, Pinky," Noodles joked.

"He said my name," Pinky gloated and sat back down.

"I never was a big talker," Noodles began. "Goodness

knows, with this guy around—" He motioned to Pinky "—who would have the time?" They all laughed, Pinky nodding in agreement.

Noodles took a big breath. "It all goes back to a wee lad I had the amazing good fortune to meet...one of the most generous, energetic, honest, and brave individuals—sit down, Pinky," he said, interrupting himself. "It's not you." Laughs all around.

"This lad made me realize it is okay to accept who I am. I'm not a talker. I only speak when I really have something important to say. I used to feel that to be accepted, one had to talk all the time." Pinky pointed to himself—as did everyone else, even Rohan now. "Believe it or not, most snakes are quite chatty. But he taught me that it's okay to just shed the snake I thought I was supposed to be...and just be me."

Pinky's hand went up.

"How did you meet this...what's his name?" Kee asked.

"Hey, I was gonna ask that!" Pinky groaned, putting his hand back down.

"Well," Noodles continued, "you would know him as Lucky."

"Oooh." Pinky squealed with excitement. "Now we're getting somewhere!"

"Shhh!" Kee and Kyle scolded.

"And the way we met...well...Pinky, you'll appreciate this." Pinky's eyes got big. "I ate him!" They all gasped.

"What?" Pinky said. "You ate a Baldi? Awesome!"

"No, no," Noodles corrected. "I never said he was a Baldi." They all stared with anticipation...and a little confusion.

"But you said he was a Lucky," Pinky said.

"He was not just any Lucky, but *the* one from which the term was first derived."

Pinky turned to Kyle. "What does derived mean?"

"Came from."

Pinky groaned. "Why doesn't he just say that?"

Noodles continued. "The funny thing about Lucky is that it's all just a mispronuncia—"

"Wait, wait, wait!" Pinky said. "There are Luckys that are *not* Baldis? Like, I could be a Lucky?"

"Yes, Pinky, you could certainly be a Lucky." Pinky smiled, puffing out his chest.

"You're not—" Noodles added with a grin, deflating Pinky "—but a mouse certainly could be." They each started to point at themselves with the same inquisitive expression on each face. "And yes, a skunk can be a Lucky…" Pinky looked even more disappointed now. "A snake…"

"Oh, come on!" Pinky said.

"And a bee." Kee and Rohan looked at each other and

smiled. "In fact, one of the reasons I am speaking at this very moment is because I believe our own Kee...*is* a Lucky." Their jaws dropped. Pinky scooted a little closer to Kee. Kyle beamed. Rohan grinned, almost knowingly.

Kee just stared, mouth still hanging open. "What... wait—" she stuttered.

"Yes?" Noodles said.

"Me? Really?" They all started to nod, suddenly realizing that it made perfect sense.

Noodles nodded. "Yes, you."

Kee was confused. "But...how...why?"

"Slow down, slow down. Don't you want to know how I met that first Lucky?"

They all nodded...except Pinky. "Not really."

"The thing is," Noodles continued, "he may be the first one we know as Lucky, but Luckys have been around us the whole time. We just don't see them. And this one just happens to be...a duck."

"Whoa," Pinky said. "You ate a whole duck?"

"Well, he was quite small at the time…an egg, in fact."

"You ate a poor, defenseless, fuzzy baby duck?" Pinky said.

Noodles nodded with a grin. "Just as quickly as I ate a poor, defenseless, fuzzy, pink baby mouse!" Pinky gulped. "And just as with mice, it turns out I cannot digest duck eggs."

"Is he still in there?" Pinky tilted his head to scan Noodles for any unforeseen lumps.

"No, Pinky, he's not still in there." Pinky looked skeptical… and a bit jealous. "The last I heard he was living on a farm down south somewhere with a good family of Baldis."

"He lives with Baldis?" Pinky said.

"Yes, they take care of him. You know, Pinky, sometimes we all need a little assistance." Noodles scooped up Pinky and put him onto his back. Pinky grinned. "Being hatched inside a snake—or, I presume that is the reason—his feet did not form quite right. No webbing. He couldn't swim or paddle…not a stroke. He could sing and dance like a fool—"

"A dancing duck?" Pinky said.

"Actually, I did see him swim once…with a dolphin."

"That's not true!" Pinky said, shaking his head. "Is it?"

"It is," Noodles said. "And it is precisely because he did all those amazing things—daring to be and do whatever he could, regardless of what others thought was possible of him—that he became such an inspiration…someone others, even non-ducks looked up to. Someone who made others just…feel better…a 'Lucky.' Or as he should be called—"

"Whoa, there she is," said a drone bee, one of two stumbling around the corner, a bit tipsy. "Hey there, honey! Get it, get it?" They both chuckled. "How *you* doin'?"

CHAPTER 13

SHEAR

Rohan jumped up from Kyle's nose. "You will have respect and address her highness as 'Your Majesty!'" Kee grabbed his wing with hers to calm him down.

"Who does this one-winged wonder think he is?" the first one stammered.

The other was staring up at Kyle in awe. "I must have had a lot more of that funky nectar than I thought. It looks like they're sitting on the nose of a skunk!" They both started laughing hysterically. The rest just stared at them in semi-amused disgust.

The first one then looked to his right and elbowed the second. "Do you see a mouse sitting on a snake over here?" They both stared at Pinky and Noodles, who were staring back, unimpressed.

"Yup," he said, reaching out to poke Noodles with an antenna. Noodles didn't move.

"Blah!" Pinky finally belted, startling the two strangers.

"Aaaaagh," they yelled. "The mouse is real!"

"And so am I!" Noodles said in a slow, threatening voice, sliding his tail around and behind the intruders.

"As am I!" Kyle spoke in a low, menacing voice, leaning down to within an inch of their faces. "And I'm feeling especially hungry for bee right now." His stomach suddenly roared, right on cue.

"Aaaaagh!" they both screamed. "What was that?"

Kee, Pinky, and Noodles all grinned, knowing it is was a bluff. "Nice touch with the tummy growl," Kee whispered.

"I didn't plan that. I actually *am* hungry."

"Of course you are." She grinned, patting him on the nose.

Rohan was getting ever more impatient with the intruders. "What are you doing here?" he said.

They looked at each other. "Uh…same as you, boss." They chuckled. "You know…just lookin' for a little…"

"Enough!" Rohan said, glaring from the tip of Kyle's nose.

"Oh, *big* bee…what are ya gonna do," the first one said, stepping a bit closer, "sting us?" They both laughed. Then they noticed Kee staring at them intently. "Or…or ya gonna have your little queen fight your battles for you?"

Kyle, Kee, Pinky, and Noodles all prepared to pounce but waited for Rohan's response. Rohan stared them straight in the eyes and spoke slowly and deliberately. "No, not *for* me—" He reached his wing back toward Kee "—*with* me!" Kee stood to join Rohan. Though smaller than all three, she still had more stinger power than the entire hive combined. Pinky, Noodles, and Kyle all grinned.

The two intruders both gulped. "Well, lucky for you, we need to get back to the hive and help…coronate a new queen, if you know what I mean."

"Aaaagh!" Rohan yelled, jumping off Kyle's nose and chasing them past the end of the booth.

"Rohan!" Kee said.

He stopped and briefly turned to reassure her. "Don't worry, my lady. Just making sure they know their way out." He then disappeared around the corner.

"Be careful!" she said…then noticed the boys staring at her, all with goofy grins. "What?" she said with a small smile. Pinky started to make kissy-face noises while hugging himself. Noodles jabbed him, knocking him over.

"Yes, I like him, okay," Kee said. "What's wrong with that?" More grins.

"Look," Noodles said, changing the subject, "we need to get you back to your hive." Pinky and Kyle nodded. "Rohan says they'll replace you soon if you don't return." Kee turned a bit solemn and quiet.

"You *are* going back, right?" Kyle asked, not sure he wanted to hear the answer. Kee looked at him but didn't respond.

"The princesses said you abandoned them," Pinky said. "But I told Rohan, no way, she would never do that! Our Kee is all about the group and keeping everyone together—" His voice softened, becoming almost tender "—like family."

"The pact," Kee said. "You remembered."

"Of course. That's why we're here...well, that and the grub." He pointed to Kyle's belly with a grin.

"Well, that's no surprise," Kee said with a giggle. "He's a walking stomach!"

Kyle nodded, looking a bit guilty. "But how did *you* end up here?" he asked. "How did you find us?"

"We thought you had—" Pinky gulped.

"On a Rumbler!" Kee said.

"What? You drove a Rumbler?"

"No, no—I got caught on the one that almost hit Kyle—well, on the arm of the Baldi inside, actually." They all stared in amazement. "He had some kind of weird outer-skin on his arm. I got tangled—"

"Oh, they all have that," Pinky said.

"The next thing I knew I was here," she continued. "And once I got my senses back, I smelled Kyle."

"What?" Kyle said with surprise. "I smell?" He blew into his paw, checking his breath.

"Yes, I am sorry to break it to you, Kyle, but you *do* still have a scent. It's not going to scare anyone away, but it did help me find you." Pinky pointed to himself and gave Kee a quizzical look. "Yes, Pinky, you smell too."

He grinned. "I know." Noodles nodded.

"And to answer your question—" Kee looked at each one of them then turned back to Kyle "—yes, I am going back."

They all nodded...though Kyle struggled to keep a brave face. "Are you sure?" he said. "I still have room on this snout for two—you know, if you and Rohan..."

She giggled, patting his nose with her wing. "Yes, I'm sure…or at least I am now. I wasn't in the beginning, though. In fact, I was pretty sure I would not go back." They all listened intently. She looked down, gathering her thoughts. "I did abandon the hive…and I'm not proud of it." They all stared in disbelief.

"I admit it. I—I was not in a happy place. I had just become queen…then, before I even had a chance to find a mate, I lost my wing. In our world—the bee world—flying is how you find a mate. The hive's future depends upon it. Then, on top of all that, as you may have noticed, I am quite…well, petite." Pinky shook his head. "Most queens are twice my size. How am I going to get the respect of the hive when I am smaller than my own workers?" The boys were hanging on every word. "So, yes, I abandoned them… but I did it to save the hive."

Pinky looked confused. "What? How—why…"

"If the queen cannot mate," she said, "the hive will die. The only way to save it is to disappear, allowing a new queen to rise to the top and take over. But, then came—"

"Rohan!" Kyle finished her sentence.

"No." She laughed. "Rohan is simply the…pollen on the anther." Blank stares all around.

"Huh?" Pinky said.

"Bee talk," Kyle whispered.

"No, then came you, Kyle," she continued, turning around on his nose to look him in the eye.

"Me?" he said, surprised.

"Yes, you, Kyle. You and your no-stinkin', grub-munchin',

bronco-buckin', blackberry-snortin'…"

Kyle laughed. "I remember. That was your fault!"
He smiled wide.

Kee walked along his snout to the very base of one of
his big, dark eyes. "You saved me," she said, holding on to
his lower lid. "You not only saved my life—multiple
times—you inspired me to live!" Her eyes started to water.
"I left my hive that morning thinking my life was over…
but then…there you were…big, wet snout in my face,
daring me to take a ride with you—*you*—a skunk!"

He sniffled a giggle, getting a bit teary now too.
"I remember."

"That…that is what I needed. Your little nudge…to
make a statement. Take control. To decide to move forward
and not waste away. That was my 'Shear.'"

"One of the dares!" Pinky said excitedly. "That's one of
the two dares, Shear and Share!"

"Actually, there are three," Kee said.

"Dares?" Kyle asked.

"I'm pretty sure it's just two," Pinky mumbled. Noodles
rolled his eyes.

"Remember the Lucky that Noodles told us about, the
duck Lucky?" Kee asked. "Well, like he said, a Baldi can be
a Lucky too. And as is typical with Baldis—"

"Wait, wait," Pinky said. "How do *you* know so much
about Baldis? I thought you had never seen one until today."

"That is true, but before I left the hive, I did have a
few thousand 'assistants' working for me who were quite
informative," she said with a smile.

"Show-off," Pinky said.

"In the Baldi world," she continued, "they always like to figure out how things work. So they figured out that becoming a Lucky happens in three stages, or 'dares.'"

"Two," Pinky whispered.

"Shear is the one where you make a defiant stand, take control, and do something symbolic that declares, 'I am taking charge and making a change.' For me, that was the moment I decided to take that ride with a strange skunk." Kyle smiled.

"And the other one," Pinky interrupted, "is 'Share,' where you tell your friends and loved ones about the tough stuff you are dealing with…or the life changes you're about to make—like when Kyle told us all about his stinkless tail."

"Exactly. That is an excellent examp—" Kee started but then noticed a pair of Baldi legs approaching. Or at least she assumed it was a Baldi. Its legs were covered with some kind of loose outer skin, similar to the kind she had seen on the Baldi's arm.

Its feet clunked on the hard floor with each step. "Well, Sally, I'm outta here," said a low, gravelly voice. "Gotta give a ride to a few million bees…some almond orchards down in California."

"Don't forget the ones you brought in with you!" she said. "See ya on the flip side." There was a slow *creak*, then *whap!*

"Well," Kee said somberly, "that's my ride." They all looked at her for a moment, not sure what to say. "So, you boys coming or what?"

CHAPTER 14

DINE AND DASH

The four of them sat behind the same sumac bush just to the left of the porch deck, scanning the gravel lot ahead. They were all still breathing heavily after a chaotic dash from under the table. They could see a Baldi walking toward a big Rumbler loaded with hundreds of white boxes. "Do you see him?" Kyle whispered to Kee.

"Who, the Baldi?" she said. "Yeah, he's right there."

"No, not the Baldi. You *know* that's not who you're looking for."

Kee turned to him. "He'll be there," she said, scanning the air with her antennae. "Rain is coming. He'll be headed back to the hive." Kyle nodded. "He'll be there," she said again, trying to reassure herself.

Pinky interrupted in a bit of a panic. "So let me see if I have this straight..." Kyle and Kee kept scanning ahead. "We're gonna run across this wide open lot, and when I say, 'we', I of course mean Kyle and 'Scoot-along' here..." gesturing to Noodles, "dodge any wandering Rumblers *and* Baldis along the way, somehow climb up *onto* a Rumbler, which we hope is the right one, then hang on for dear life as we careen at a speed that...that Noodles couldn't imagine in his wildest dreams, all to head to some place no one has ever heard of...Kaflorna? Do I have that about right?" He was breathing so heavily now, he had to sit down and rest.

Kee ignored Pinky, focusing on the Baldi. "He's almost there. We better hurry."

"What?" Pinky shook his head. "Oh, and let me add to all that," he gasped, "we better hurry! I think I'm going to throw up." He put a hand over his mouth and another on his tummy.

"You're gonna be fine," Kee assured him. "Ready?"

"Ready? READY?" Pinky said. "Are you kidding? She's kidding, right?" he begged, looking at the other two, who were also ignoring him. "I mean, we obviously are not ready until I am safely tucked away inside—NOODLES!" Pinky yelled, seeing the three of them suddenly bolt out of the bush. Noodles snagged Pinky at the last second with the tip of his tail and flung him into the air. "Aaaaaagh!" Pinky screamed. "What—is—happeniiiing?"

Noodles surged forward, catching Pinky in his mouth just before hitting the ground. "Noodles! I swear to—" he started to berate but was cut short as Noodles quickly swallowed.

Kyle zigged and zagged across the gravel lot, stopping momentarily behind a stationary Rumbler before dashing forward again. Kee could just see the last foot of the Baldi disappear inside the Rumbler. There was a small shake, a huge rumble, then two plumes of smoke shot out from the vertical appendages on each side of its big, boxy head.

"Faster, Kyle!" Kee said, hanging on with all six legs and both antennae.

Meanwhile, Pinky was continuing to hamper Noodles' progress by randomly throwing open his jaw to look out, momentarily blinding Noodles and bringing them both to a stop. Kee looked back but couldn't see either of them. "Where are they?"

Kyle stopped to catch his breath. "Shall I wait?" Another great rumble was heard and they could see their soon-to-be ride slowly start to move.

"No, no," Kee yelled, also out of breath. "Maybe they're hiding under one of them. Keep going!"

The Rumbler made a slow right turn as it appeared to be circling the lot before exiting. Kyle, anticipating its path, dashed left to catch it on the way out. Kee looked back. No Noodles.

A couple of Rumblers behind, Noodles was preoccupied with Pinky, who had just thrown his jaw open again. This time Noodles was ready. Just as his jaw opened, Noodles squeezed and pushed him with his tongue, ejecting Pinky out of his mouth. *Plop!* A wet ball of fur shot out onto the gravel in front of him.

"Hey! What do you think you're doin—" Pinky started

to yell, but before he could finish, Noodles scooped him up again with the tip of his tail, this time flipping him onto his back. "Aaaaaagh!" Pinky was lying face down on his tummy, hugging both sides of Noodles with all four legs. "It's going the other way!" he said as the Rumbler disappeared to his right. Pinky dropped his face onto Noodles' back in frustration. "We're gonna die. We're gonna die. We're gonna die."

Noodles shot left past a sleeping Rumbler then straight toward the side of another. "What are you doing? What are you doing? What are you—aaaaaagh!" Pinky buried his face in Noodles' back as they slid under the Rumbler and out the other side. Pinky's tiny paws were embedded in Noodles' sides.

Kyle stopped behind the last Rumbler in the lot, waiting for his opportunity. "What are you going to do?" Kee said. "How are you going to get on?"

Kyle watched intently as it approached. "Here it comes," he said to himself, ignoring Kee in order to focus.

"Here it comes!" Kee said, just as the front was passing them. "Kyle?"

"And here—we—GO!" Kyle bolted to his right.

"Aaaaaagh!" Kee yelled, losing grip on her three right feet and now dangling down the left side of Kyle's snout. The back of the Rumbler was about to pass. "We're missing it, we're missing it!" She pulled herself back onto his snout and suddenly noticed a strap dangling down the side. "Yes...yes!"

Kyle lunged at the strap, just catching the edge with his

teeth. He wrapped four limbs and tail around the strap and then grabbed again with his teeth on a spot slightly higher. The Rumbler bucked and kicked out of the lot onto smooth Rumbler tracks and started to accelerate.

Kee looked back, scanning the lot for Noodles and Pinky as Kyle continued shimmying up the strap. "They didn't make it! They didn't ma…" Suddenly something grabbed Kyle's left leg, almost pulling him off the strap. He looked down. "Noodles!" Kee yelled with delight. "And…and Pinky?" She noticed a trembling Pinky, eyes closed, on the *outside* of Noodles, clinging to the very tip of his tail. "The gang's all here!"

CHAPTER 15

MY HIVE

Kyle was lying flat on his back, gazing up at passing clouds from the tail of a speeding Rumbler. Kee lay on his chest, rising and falling with his every breath. The wind *whooshed* by, causing the big net between them and the stacks of hives to make a steady *flop-flop-flop* as it undulated back and forth.

Noodles was busy trying to keep an overly excited Pinky from falling over the edge. "This is so awesome!" Pinky yelled with a huge grin. "We are on a Rumbler!" he said, giggling uncontrollably. "We are actually on a Ruuuum-blllll-errrrrr!" He leaned over the side until the wind whipped his whiskers. "Woooo-hoooo!" he squealed, reaching his arms over his head. The situation was making Noodles a bit tense as he gripped Pinky tightly by the tail.

The other end of Noodles looped around an eyelet in the net behind Kyle.

Kee giggled. "Look at him. He is so happy right now!" Kyle looked up to see Pinky and started to giggle as well. They both just sat and watched Pinky's pure joy for several minutes.

Kyle imagined what could be going through Pinky's head. "This is probably a dream of his...you know, overpowering a big, bad Baldi, conquering his savage Rumbler, and then riding it victoriously back to...the Kingdom of Pinkies."

"Where it rains grubs!" Kee added. They both laughed as Pinky switched between giggling one second and then screaming with delight the next.

"Yeee-haaaw!" he yelled as a gust of wind almost yanked him out of Noodles' grip.

Kee lay back down on Kyle's chest to look at the clouds, reaching all six of her feet straight up, as if trying to touch them. "I have to admit, I'm a bit envious of him right now..." She paused, lost in the clouds. "He's flying!" Kyle looked down to see her flapping her one wing. "I would so have loved to fly...just once. Oh, the places I would go. The things I would do."

Kyle watched as she mimed with her feet and wing as if running, jumping, and then soaring through space. A grin came over his face. "So," he asked tenderly, "what *would* you do if you had both wings? Tell me."

Kee laughed. "Ha, what *wouldn't* I do!" She thought for a second.

"I'd go faster than fast…and higher than high.
I'd fly loops upside down and around in the
sky." She was standing now.

"I'd go places so far, not like this place at all.
With magical Pinkies that grow six feet tall!"
Kyle laughed.

"I'd swim with Duck Lucky…and dolphins, no
fear." She turned to Kyle. "Then bring all I've
learned, right back home, to you, here."

Kyle smiled, a little teary, picked up Kee, and set her on
his nose. "Well," he said, a bit choked up, "we better make
that happen then." Kee smiled. "Goodness knows I have a
lot to learn!"

Just then a familiar face popped through a hole near the
bottom of the net. "You folks enjoying your ride?" said a
rugged voice.

"Rohan!" Kee squealed with delight, almost falling off
Kyle's nose. She gestured to Kyle to move closer. "You made it!"

Noodles, hearing the commotion, reeled in Pinky and
slithered over to join them.

"I did indeed," Rohan said in a quiet voice, looking around
behind him.

"What's wrong?" Kee whispered.

"It's those two vile, aspiring queens…" He hesitated, looking behind again. "They're…they could emerge any second. And once they do, they could have followers… you know, those who would not exactly welcome a former queen with open arms?" The boys looked at each other, a bit worried now. "If you still want to do this, we need to get you there before the other queens hatch." He paused, trying to think of another option. He leaned in to Kee. "Look, we don't have to do this. You have nothing to prove. We could leave now and they would be—"

"No!" Kee said, abruptly stopping him. "*I* am their queen. I may be small…and a bit less mobile—" waving her one wing "—but that is *my* hive." She stopped, catching herself. "*Our* hive." She then got a very stern and determined look on her face. "If they want it…they're going to have to take it!"

Rohan swallowed the lump in his throat. "Okay, but you need to get there now." Kee nodded. "You go ahead," he continued. "I'll be right behind you." Kyle raised his paw to his nose so he could lower Kee down. "I just need to let these guys know—" Rohan started to say, but was cut short by Kee, who was now suspicious.

"What?" Kee asked, stopping abruptly. "What is it you *need* to let them know? Whatever you need to tell them, you can tell me."

"Uhhh—" Rohan stammered, caught off guard.

Kee was more confrontational than they had seen before. "Here's an idea," she said, spinning around on Kyle's paw and defiantly stepping back onto his nose. "You tell them whatever you like. I just need to tell Kyle something first."

Kyle gulped as his eyes opened wide.

A sweet but determined expression now came over Kee's face. "Kyle?" she said. He stared nervously. "Kyle!" she yelled.

"Y-yes, yes…I'm listening," he stuttered sheepishly.

"You better be, mister." The other three guys started to slowly back away. "Don't—you—move…any of you!" Kee turned briefly to catch them. "Kyle," she continued, looking him in the eye, "do not…under any circumstances try to come help." Kyle stared straight ahead. "What did I just say?"

"Uh—uh…under—no—cir—cir—" He looked around nervously to the guys for assistance.

"Circus pants!" Pinky whispered proudly. Noodles slapped him in the head with his tail. "What? That's not it?" he said, looking confused.

Kee's eyes were locked on Kyle now. "Say it with me. Cir—cum—stances," they both mouthed together.

"Circumstances. Got it," Kyle said on his own now. "Under no circumstances—uh—to help—go help—I mean no help. I don't go help. I no help."

Pinky nodded his head and patted him on the foot. "You're doing great!" he whispered, rolling his eyes.

Kee stopped and probed the air with her antennae. "Do you smell that?" Pinky sniffed. Noodles' tongue darted around. Rohan wiggled his antennae. Kyle just looked confused. "That's rain. Rain is coming," she said menacingly. "We bees do not like rain. We get very grumpy when it rains."

"Oh, great," Rohan mumbled.

"I heard that, Rohan!" Kee sneered. He smiled a big, guilty smile. "We have over fifty thousand in just our hive alone. And they loooove to sting in packs." They all gulped. "So if you, for some reason, lose your mind and decide to be—heroic—to help the 'damsel in distress—'" Kee made quotes with her antennae "—you will be killed." Kyle gulped again. "Remember that one *little* sting I gave you?" Kyle put his paw up to a still slightly swollen eye. "The one that jolted you to the side of the road? You got it?" Kyle nodded, quite frightened now…but more so by Kee at this moment than the other bees. "You got it?" she yelled. Kyle nodded vigorously. "And that goes for the rest of you, too." Rohan pointed at the rest of them. "You too, Rohan!" she yelled without even looking at him. He flashed a nervous grin. "I will see *you*—" she turned to Rohan directly now "—at the hive in five minutes." She then scrambled down Kyle's arm and disappeared around the corner.

Pinky sighed. "Whew!" They all started to chuckle nervously. "That was a close—" Kee popped her head around the corner for one last glare. They stopped and she departed.

Kyle looked around one more time to make sure she was really gone then leaned in to Rohan. "What do you know? What are you not telling her?" Rohan stared. "I could see it in your eyes. What is it?"

Rohan hesitated for a moment then spoke in a very grim tone. "They're huge!" The boys looked at each other. "The two queens…even before they've hatched, you can see how massive and wicked they are."

Kyle looked confused. "How big are they? Twice her size?" he asked, but not sure he wanted to hear the answer.

"No," Rohan responded. "Twice *my* size."

CHAPTER 16

THE BIG STING

Kee scurried along the inside of the net toward the front of the Rumbler. Random drones from other hives kept buzzing her along the way—"Hi there"—"Howdy!"—"How *you* doin'?"—but she ignored them, focused on getting to *her* hive as soon as possible.

The weight of the task before her was starting to sink in. Although she could talk a big talk, Kee knew that Rohan was ultimately right. If she were to have any chance of keeping the hive (and her life, for that matter), she must get there before the other two virgin queens hatched.

You see, Kee was just one of three princesses in line for the crown—sisters, specifically selected by their dying queen as potential successors, knowing it would be up to each to determine who actually became the new queen. The method of deciding which of the three would be simple and the same as has always been: fight to the death, winner take all.

Typically, that fight goes pretty quickly. The first one out stings and kills the others while still in their brood cells, before they ever hatch. This was the dilemma now before Kee: how to muster the courage to kill both queens…while they slept.

"What am I doing? WHAT AM I DOING?" Kee started to question herself as she approached the stack of hives where hers was perched—at the very top. *Okay, okay, this is simple. You can do this,* she thought, trying to convince herself. *They would certainly kill me, without hesitation, if the roles were reversed. Yet, here I am, all hesitation!* Kee groaned, climbing past the first two hives, more foreign drones harassing her all the way—"Howdy"— "Hey there"—"How *you* doin?"

"Seriously?" she said, grumbling to herself while continuing to climb. "Is there not an original thought among a single one of you?" She looked back and sighed. *Where's Rohan?*

Come to think of it, would I even be doing this if I hadn't found Rohan? How would I continue the hive? Would I have to accept one of these losers? I think I'd rather sit on my own stinger!

Kee trudged past two more boxes, finally reaching her hive. She now saw drones that were familiar to her. "Kee!" said one with excitement. "Where have you been…and how *you* do—"

"Not now, Ralph!" she said, cutting him off abruptly and heading straight for the entrance. As she got to the doorway, she stopped to gather her thoughts. *Well, it's now or never.* And with that, she took a big breath and walked through a small opening at the bottom of the hive.

"Queen Kee! Queen Kee!" squealed several workers as she passed. "You're back!" yelled another, both excited and confused. The news of Kee's return spread quickly throughout the hive, creating an oddly festive yet foreboding atmosphere. Squeals of joy quickly turned to gasps of fear.

No sooner had Kee passed the first row of combs than she felt it—a sudden dynamic change in the hive. She could smell it, too. The entire tone of the hive was changing. That could only mean one thing: the queens had started to hatch.

Kee started running ever faster now toward the queen cells. "My queen! My queen!" greeted a couple more workers. "Please, my queen, don't go in there!" warned one. "No, my queen, no!" pleaded another. Kee scurried still faster. *Maybe I can get there before they completely emerge and dry off.* "The queen! The queen!" came more shouts of joy and confusion from nearby workers. "No, Queen Kee, don't! They're too big!"

Kee took one last breath and rounded the corner to the queen cells, where she stopped in her tracks. They were both empty.

"Queen Kee," she suddenly heard from behind her in a deep, menacing voice. "Welcome back." Kee spun around to see a creature so huge, she had to look almost straight up to see her face. Kee started to hyperventilate but quickly spun around again, looking for the other.

"Where—" she gulped, trying to get the words out. "Where is she?"

"Where is who?" the giant queen responded in a slow and haunting voice. "Oh, you mean the other wannabe? We don't need her now, do we?" She paused, her raspy speech seeming to strain with each syllable. "So I killed her!"

Workers in and around the queen cells were shaking. Kee kept looking around. "Where—where is the body?" she managed to get out, not trusting her. *And where is Rohan?*

"Oh, that," the wicked queen said with a hiss. "Funny thing about young, pristine, tender, juicy queens like us, Kee—you know, nursed on a diet of pure Royal Jelly and all—" She licked her jagged lips as a small drop of drool started to form at the corner of her dark, crooked mouth. Kee was trembling. "We," she continued, carefully enunciating every last syllable, "we can be quite—" She grinned a most sinister grin, then her tone got even deeper. "Quite tasty!"

Kee stumbled toward the combs behind her, but a couple of evil-looking workers shoved her back. "But you! Look at you with your *one* wing," the dark queen said, poking at Kee with one of her spiny antennae. "You're barely as big as a worker, hardly a nibble." She chuckled a slow, demonic sort of chuckle.

The two evil workers laughed as well and approached Kee, mocking her. "Ooh, look at us," one said. "Which one of us is the queen?"

"Oh, I'm the queen!" said the other.

"No, I'm the queen!" said the first, taking turns poking Kee with their antennae. "Look at me. I'm Kee, and I can't snag a drone 'cuz I can't fly." The two chuckled, each flapping one wing. One wandered over to a nearby drone watching from the side. "Hi there, big boy," she said, pretending to flirt. "Take off a wing and stay awhile." They both rolled on their sides with laughter.

"Stop!" Kee yelled suddenly, startling both of them.

They looked at each other and giggled. "Oh, looky here. Look who thinks she's the big—" one of them started to say, but then Kee raised her stinger and quickly stared her down.

"Uh—I—uh," the first one muttered, "I—I've got brood combs to go clean." And with that she bolted around the corner and out of sight. Kee turned to the other. "Uh—and I am supposed to help her," said the second, running after.

The wicked queen laughed. "Ha ha ha, Kee. Well done."

Kee turned to face the beast. "You're next!" she responded calmly but forcefully.

The evil queen roared with laughter. "Oh my—I like that. You *are* a spunky one!" She chuckled, briefly enjoying her little opponent before changing to a much more ominous tone. "But not wise. I am bigger, stronger—" she started but then caught herself, noticing the eyes of thousands of disgruntled workers watching her.

The entire hive had gathered and was carefully monitoring every move. The wicked queen looked around, saw each face peeking through the combs with expressions of both fear *and* anger, and moderated her tone. "Look," she said, trying to sound compassionate, "let's not make this ugly. I'll tell you what. I can be nice. You take your little wing there,

spin yourself around, head out the door, never to return—"
She paused, her voice becoming sinister once again "—and
I'll let you and all your little friends here *live!*"

"NO!" Kee replied immediately. "I've already tried that.
It didn't stick. This is my hive—*our* hive!" She looked out
at the surrounding workers, now creeping slowly out of the
combs, inspired by Kee. "I left them once—" She looked at
the thousands of hopeful faces "—I'm not doing it again."
The dark queen stared, at first in bemused amazement, but
then with growing anger.

"I'll tell *you* what," Kee continued. "Why don't *you* leave,
never to return, and I won't kill *you!* You want this hive?
You want to be queen of this hive? You're gonna have to
take it!" A brief cheer erupted around the hive until the evil
queen whipped her head around, staring down each and
every worker.

"Oh really," she uttered in a very foul tone. "As I said
before, you may be spunky, but you, my dear, are not wise.
How do you think you can possibly out-sting someone five
times your own size?" She was yelling now, her anger and
impatience finally starting to bubble over. "Even—even if
by some miracle, you found some extraordinary means by
which to kill *me*—" She looked at the cowering faces all
around. "I find it impossible to imagine you being fortunate
enough to kill—" She paused as a dark grin came over her
face "—both of us!"

The other wicked queen, even larger and more menacing
than the first, suddenly dropped from above to shrieks

throughout the hive. Two enormous, dark, spiny creatures now bore down on Kee from both sides. Kee lifted her stinger, spinning to the right, then the left, then back again. "Now, Queen Kee," said the first, "is that any way to welcome family?" The two beasts looked at each other and grinned. "Any last words?"

Suddenly the sky opened up. The top of the hive flew off and a furry black-and-white face peeked in.

"Kyle, no!" Kee screamed. A clap of thunder crashed, and huge drops started to descend from the dark clouds above. Kyle looked over at Rohan, who was sitting on the top edge of the hive, directing. Kyle grabbed the middle frame of combs, yanking it straight out of the hive, pulling Kee, the two evil queens, and several hundred workers with it.

The first wicked queen roiled with rage. "You have messed with the wrong hive, my stinky friend. Prepare to die!" she yelled, signaling to the workers. "You know what to do, ladies. Go get—" But before she could finish, Kyle opened his mouth, drove his snout straight down at both queens, chomped down, and swallowed. "KYLE!" Kee cried.

Dizzy with pain from multiple internal stings, Kyle fell backward, dropping the frame back into the hive. Noodles lowered the top back onto the hive as the deluge commenced. Any bees crazy or stupid enough to have left were now dead or back inside.

CHAPTER 17

SHED

K yle lay on his back, eyes closed, on top of a stack of hives. Rain continued to pummel his face and chest.

"Are you sure he's not going to drown out there?" Kee asked from within the relatively dry shelter of Noodles' mouth. Noodles lay on the same stack of hives surrounding Kyle, mouth agape with three rain-soaked friends inside.

"I think he's fine," replied Pinky from his cramped, snuggly space between Kee and Rohan. "The rain might even wake him up quicker."

"I can still see him breathing," Rohan said. Noodles closed his eyes, enjoying the rhythmic massage of the rain on his back, almost oblivious to the three compadres huddled within his lower jaw.

Suddenly the rain disappeared, as did the sky. The

Rumbler came to a stop under some kind of shelter. Kee turned to Rohan. "I'm gonna check on Kyle. Can you—"

"Check on the hive?" Rohan said. "I'm on it." He smiled and headed down below.

Kee popped out of Noodles' mouth and scurried over to Kyle. "Kyle. Kyle!" she yelled, climbing onto his vertical snout. She slid down and pried open his left eye. "Helloooooo. Hellooooo in there."

"Aaaaagh!" Kyle blurted, suddenly snapping out of it. "Why do you always do that?" Kee smiled and hugged the bridge of his nose. Kyle smiled back—as did the boys.

"I told you he was fine!" Pinky hollered.

Kee was still locked in a six-legged hug on Kyle's nose when she started to question him in her pretend scolding voice. "What did I *tell* you?"

"What?" he responded in his pretend oblivious voice. "What did I do?"

"You ate a couple massively disgusting bees, that's what!" Pinky said, running up from the side. Kyle, suddenly recalling the incident, turned green and started to dry-heave.

"Pinky!" Kee said.

"What? I'm proud of him." Kee glared. "Too soon?" he added, backing away from the barf zone. Kee stroked Kyle's nose with her wing, hanging on tightly with all six legs so as not to get thrown as he gagged. Noodles looked at Pinky and just shook his head.

Kyle's heaves subsided and he lay down, sweat dripping from the side of his head. "You okay?" Kee asked tenderly. Kyle nodded then turned to give Pinky a look.

Pinky sat there with a guilty grin. "Sorry. It *was* really impressive the way you—" Kee shot him another look.

She turned back to Kyle. "How are the stings? Still sore?" Kyle had a small gag again. "Oh, sorry!" She continued to stroke his nose. "Just lie here and think of…" she started but was distracted by Pinky, who had a nervous look. *What is he up to?*

Suddenly Pinky darted toward Kyle, throwing himself at his paws. "Hold me!"

"What?" Kyle said, moving his paws away from Pinky.

"What are you doing?" Kee said.

"Hold me. Hold me with your paws," Pinky said again, trying to grab Kyle's paws and move them closer.

"Pinky!" Kee yelled.

"It helps! It does. It always helped my Baldi. Whenever she got sick, she would hold me in her hands and rub my back with her fingers—" Pinky started to get a little emotional.

"Your Baldi?" Kee asked. "The one you mentioned earlier? Your Lucky?"

"Yes, yes. She—it just helps. Try. Just try it," Pinky pleaded.

Kyle looked at Kee, who at first gave him a shrug, then the go-ahead nod. Kyle slowly moved his front paws closer to Pinky, who grabbed them and pulled them onto his sides. Kyle looked anxiously at Kee.

"Anything?" Pinky said.

Kyle stared at Kee, a bit dumbfounded. "Uh—no—not yet."

"I think it takes a few minutes. Rub my head," Pinky suggested.

"What?" Kyle started to protest, but then Kee gestured to go ahead.

"Just use your thumbs," Pinky said.

"Could you lift him up so I can see?" Kee asked.

"Yeah, yeah. Good idea. I think I need to be in the air. She always held me up by her face."

Kyle groaned, rolling his eyes as he awkwardly stroked the back of Pinky's head. "This is just weird."

Kee watched Pinky's eyes close, and a small grin started to form as he drifted to another place. "Oh my gosh, look." Kee turned to Kyle, but then noticed that he too was starting to calm. Through the sensitive hairs on her feet, she could feel his pulse and respiration slow. She could even smell his stress start to melt away as his eyelids got heavy. Then, just before closing, he got a peek of Kee staring at him, a big smile on her face.

"Okay, that's enough." Kyle opened his eyes and set Pinky down.

"Wait—what?" Pinky asked. "Did it work? Did you feel it? It worked, didn't it?"

"Uh—I—I don't know," Kyle mumbled. Kee nodded with a grin.

"How did you do that?" she asked.

"I don't know," Pinky said, lying on his back. "Just whenever she—my Lucky—would start going through her—her—"

"Her what, Pinky?" Kee said. Noodles slid his tail around Pinky then nudged him to continue.

"You were right," Pinky said.

"I was? I mean, of course I was!" Kee said with a sly grin. Kyle rolled his eyes. "But uh—just to be clear—which thing was I right about this time?"

"The dares. There are three."

"Oh right, the Shed Dare."

"Whenever she went through the hardest part of her Shed," Pinky continued, "the part where they bring in the shiny, leafless tree with the strange baby Rumblers on every branch—well, they really tweet more than rumble—and their flashing eyes and long, long tongues…"

"Wait, wait," Kyle interrupted. "Shiny tree? Baby Rumblers?" He then whispered to Kee, "And what's the shed thingy again?"

"Hey Pinky," Kee said, "we would love to hear about the tree and baby Rumblers, but first, Kyle is still not quite sure about the—what did you call it—the 'shed thingy.' What is a shed thingy?"

"Hey, I whispered that!"

"Oh right, right," Pinky said, excited to explain. "Well, you know there is the Share Dare, where you tell others about some problem you are dealing with—"

"Like Kee's wing and size insecurities?" Kyle said, grinning at Kee.

"Laugh it up, big boy," she warned with a grin of her own.

"Yes, exactly," Pinky continued. "Then there is Shear—"

"Yeah, yeah," Kee interrupted. "Where you do something symbolically defiant to show you intend to beat the problem. Like when I dared to take a ride with a stinkless, bee-nauseated skunk," she said with another grin. Kyle laughed.

"Yes, yes, perfect. Which brings me to the Shed Dare, which is—"

"Ooh, shed is my favorite," Noodles said. They all grinned.

"No kidding." Pinky giggled. "Why don't you explain this one then, Mr. Talkative."

"Well, the Shed Dare," Noodles started explaining, to everyone's delight, "is all about growth, transformation… and the challenges we endure to get there."

"Smaller words, please," Pinky said. "For Kyle," he whispered with a grin.

"It's about letting go of your old self, along with any accompanying… 'creepers'… discarding the creepers and embracing a new, reborn self."

"Like when Kee got past her fears and confronted those evil queens," Kyle said with a smile.

"That was so awesome!" Pinky said. Kee grinned.

Kyle looked in Kee's eyes and whispered with pride, "You're the queen." She grinned and nodded. "You did it!"

"No, *you* did it," she said. "The way you tore the top off the hive and…"

"*We* did it," he said, looking around. Kee nodded.

"Yes, we did," she added, smiling at the three of them. "Thank you…thank you so much. I couldn't have…"

"Yeah, yeah, we're all the greatest," Pinky chimed in. "But isn't there a little something…or someone you're forgetting?"

"Rohan!" Kee said. "Oh my, yes, yes….dear Rohan…" she added, scurrying off Kyle's nose. "I really should be getting to…I mean, it's important that I…"

"Just go already!" Pinky said with a grin. "Wouldn't want anyone to ever say Pinky got in the way of a honeymoon."

"Thank you…thank you so…" she yelled, disappearing into the hive.

"Say 'hi' to Rohan for us," Kyle said.

"And 'bye,'" Pinky whispered. "Poor sucker." Noodles slapped him.

The Rumbler started moving again, exposing the boys to more pummeling rain. With nowhere to hide, Kyle simply lay on his stomach, head hanging over the rear edge of the hive. Pinky jumped into Noodles' mouth.

The steady hum of rain and vibrations from the Rumbler made eyelids heavy very quickly. Add to that their level of exhaustion from the day's adventures, and sleep came almost immediately.

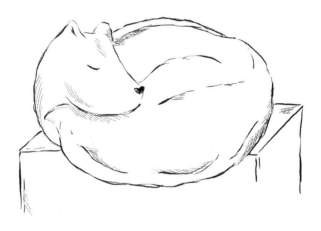

CHAPTER 18

LIFT

The Rumbler continued throughout the night. As the sun crested the eastern hills, the gang found themselves surrounded by rows and rows of beautiful almond orchards.

Kee emerged from the hive to see Pinky sitting on Kyle's nose, hanging out over the edge of the Rumbler, once again catching wind in his whiskers. "Woooo-hooooo!" he squealed as a sudden puff of wind caught his lips, inflating his mouth like a balloon and almost tipping him over. Giggling, he quickly dropped on his belly, four legs spread akimbo and head leaning over the end of Kyle's snout. Kyle laughed. "Ooh, you got any room in there?" Pinky stared directly into Kyle's semi-open mouth.

"Get outta there!" Kyle said.

Kee wandered over to Noodles, who was watching them while sunbathing on a stack of hives. "Not safe," he mumbled, shaking his head. "Not safe at all. Leaning out there like that...one bump or gust and—"

"Wee-heeeeee!" Kyle yelled, holding a paw out to catch the wind.

"Kids!" Noodles said with a smile.

Kee watched Noodles as he worried over the boys' antics. "Ya know," she whispered, leaning in close, "there's a word for someone who spends as much time thinking about and caring for those around him as you do..." Noodles barely listened, too focused on the horseplay of a mouse and skunk. "Queen." Noodles gave a distracted grin. "I mean—if you don't mind me saying so—the way you look after the boys, and after me for that matter, is almost...maternal." Noodles nodded, slightly suspicious of where this was going. They both sat quietly watching the guys.

"May I ask you something else?" Kee said. Noodles didn't budge. Kee leaned in again and whispered, "What is your real name?" Noodles turned and looked at Kee as if caught. Kee didn't flinch, continuing to stare in the direction of the two boys. "Pinky is the one who named you Noodles." A slight grin started to creep up the corners of his mouth. "But seems to me you were around well before you met Pinky."

Realizing that she knew, Noodles sighed and gave her a big smile. "Imme. My name is Imme." Kee turned and smiled.

"Hmm, interesting," she said. "That is a very...pretty name."

"Thank you," Imme said as they both laughed, sharing a

connection and understanding now that went beyond mere travel buddies.

Kee looked at Pinky and giggled to herself. "He has no idea, does he?" Imme smiled and shook her head. "Well, good for Pinky," Kee continued. "He needs a good mom like you...though he'd never admit it!" They both smiled as Kee put her wing on Imme. "I knew there was something I liked about you."

They both turned to watch the boys giggling at the edge of the speeding Rumbler. "I hate to say it," Kee said, "but Pinky was right." Imme's eyes raised. "Sometimes life gives you snake." They both smiled.

The Rumbler suddenly slowed, pulling onto a gravel road that sliced thru acres of almond trees. A farmhouse and small pond sat at the end of a long gravel driveway.

"Is this it? Is this it?" Pinky yelled, jumping up and down. He scrambled down Kyle's back and over to Imme and Kee.

"I think it might be," Kee said, looking around.

Kyle noticed Kee and Imme sitting together, suspiciously smiley. "So...is everything okay?" Kee giggled and nodded. "You sure?"

Kee knew what he was referring to. "Yes, I am fine. And he...he was a good drone."

Just then Pinky barged in, oblivious as usual. "So, how was the honeymoon?" Imme and Kyle both slapped him. Kee just smiled. Pinky, suddenly realizing his mistake, looked down out of respect... and to hide his childish grin.

The Rumbler came to a stop next to a large pond, lined with cattails and scattered with small patches of water lily.

A couple of ducks bobbed up and down as circular ripples radiated past from a recent splash. Small, bright green frogs could be seen jumping between lily pads. Kyle licked his lips. *Mmm, juicy*, he thought.

"So, shall we take a look around and see—" Kee started to say but was interrupted by a loud grumble from Kyle's tummy. "Or better yet..." They all looked at her with the same thought.

"Grub run!" they all yelled at once—except for Kyle, who yelled, "Frogs!"

They each climbed, slithered, or rode down off the Rumbler and wandered toward the edge of the pond. "You know the best way to find grubs?" Imme said. "Follow the ducks. They are excelle—" Imme stopped in midsentence as Kyle suddenly pointed to one of the ducks waddling nearby....missing the webbing on his feet.

"Uh, guys...do you see what I see?" Pinky said.

Imme set Pinky down and started to slither toward the

duck—slowly at first, then much faster. "Lockie?" she said. "Locks?" Kee and the boys froze, looking on in amazement.

"Is that—" Kee mumbled.

Pinky shrugged. "Did he say Lucky or Lockie?"

The duck, apparently not hearing her at first, still faced the pond as Imme bore down on him, moving so fast now that a collision was inevitable. "LOCKIE!"

"Mum?" the duck finally muttered, turning just before being tackled by a squealing Imme.

"MUM!" he yelled as the two tumbled down the bank, landing in a giggling pile of feathers and mud at the edge of the water.

"Lockie!" Imme squealed with joy, wrapping herself around him as they both splashed and laughed with excitement. She hung on so tightly, his eyes started to bulge.

"Too tight, Mum, too tight!" Lockie said with a gasp.

"Ooh, sorry, sorry." They both giggled.

Kyle watched, as did the other two, mouths hanging open with an expression somewhere between happy and confused. "Have we been saying it wrong the whole time?" Kyle said. Kee shrugged.

"I can't understand a thing that comes out of Noodles' mouth," Pinky said.

Kee and Kyle looked at each other and giggled. "Neither can we."

"Ha, ha…very funny. I get it!"

Imme and Lockie continued to chat and hug for several minutes, not realizing the others were still standing there.

"Oh, oops," Imme finally said, noticing three smiling faces staring at them. "Come on, Lockie, I want you to meet my new best friends." Lockie shook off the water and followed Imme—corralled by her vigilant tail—back up the bank.

"Everyone," Imme said, "this is Lockie. Lockie, this is Pinky, Kyle, and our queen bee, Kee."

"Sounds to me like she's the queen of everything," Lockie said.

"Ooh, I like that," Pinky said. Kee smiled.

Lockie reached out a wing to each of them. "Hi Pinky, Kyle, and—" He turned back to Kee "—Your Majesty." He bowed, one wing on his back and the other on his chest.

"Oh, stop it!" Kee giggled.

Imme smiled, shaking her head. "He's such a ham!"

Lockie just grinned. "Ya know," he said, speaking softly and directly to Kee, "I'd love to take you for a swim and show you around the pond, but—" He shook one of his feet "—can't swim." They all giggled. He then looked up, scanning the bright blue morning sky. "I can fly, though. Care for a ride?"

CHAPTER 19

SLEEP

Kyle looked up and smiled, his nose tingling with delight. So tingly was his nose. It just tingled and tingled. That was how happy he was for Kee. Then his nose tingled some more and—Kyle's right hand suddenly reached for his face, touching something soft and squirmy. His eyelids snapped open as he tried to focus on a fidgety pink creature staring at him from the tip of his nose. Panicked and disoriented, he quickly swiped it from his face, almost knocking it to the floor but catching the baby mouse at the last second. *Whew, that was close*, he thought. "Sorry, little buddy."

Trying to regain his surroundings, he glanced right to see his sister in bed and Mom in a chair, both with mouths wide open, sound asleep. He then heard a loud snoring coming from the chair to his left. *When did Dad get here?* "Yikes," he murmured, looking at his watch. "Well, brilliant storytelling, Kyle," he mocked himself with a grin. "Just loved it. We hung on every word! And the way you did those voices…"

He turned back to his right and patted his sister on the head. *Sleep well, sis. We'll do it again tomorrow.*

NOTES FROM THE PASTURE:
THE SCIENCE AND TRIVIA
OF BALDILOCKS

I don't know about you, but I've always been fascinated by the
behind-the-scenes thoughts and processes that go into any
creative work. I am also a bit of a science geek, so I had a pretty
good time researching and exploring the wonderful world of bees
and other creatures featured in *Baldilocks and the Three Dares*.

I also like to share. Below are some of the science notes,
thought processes, and obscure references behind the
writing of this book. *Chapter Notes* and musings are listed
in chapter order and labeled with one or more of the
following categories: *Science*, *Story Development*, and *Trivia*.

CHAPTER NOTES
SPOILER ALERT: The following notes contain spoilers
(information that will give away key points of the story,
meant to be surprises).

DO NOT READ until you have already finished the story.

KEY:

Science	Story Development	Trivia

CHAPTER 1 - MORNING NEW

Queen, Worker, and Drone

Honeybees can be classified into three main roles: queen, worker, and drone. All male honeybees are called drones and have but one purpose, to mate with the queen. All female honeybees (except the queen) are called workers and have various subroles they perform, from housekeepers to foragers. The queen is the only fertile female honeybee, and her role is to reproduce (Honey Bee - Apis mellifera, n.d.).

Creepers and DWV

The "Creepers," first mentioned in Chapter 1, are based on Varroa mites that transmit "Deformed Wing Virus" (DWV). This can be a serious setback not only for any bee that has it, often shortening its life to less than forty-eight hours, but a threat to the entire hive, causing colony collapse.

Discover more info on DWV, Varroa mites, and all kinds of cool things about honeybees here (Wilson-Rich, 2014, p. 135) and here (Williams, 2017) and maybe even here (Finley & Buford, 2016).

Predator/Prey

Coming face-to-face with a skunk is not something a bee typically looks forward to. Skunks are natural predators and typically eat honeybees (Wilson-Rich, 2014, p. 81).

Flightless Queen

When our queen "...cried 'til she filled up her bed" after learning she had lost a wing, the reason this was so upsetting to Kee is because queen bees are only effective if they can mate, which is typically done with the male drones in midair. If she cannot fly, she likely cannot mate, which means no new fertilized eggs, leading to the death of the entire hive. In such a situation, the queen would typically leave the hive, making room for another queen to take over (Webster, 2013, p. 50).

Naming Kee

This is simply a shortened version of Kira, the incredibly brave thirteen-year-old Scottish girl I met at Dreamflight and who is the inspiration for this book.

I briefly considered spelling her name as "Ki," which seems a little cooler and more obviously short for Kira; Ki is also the Sumerian goddess of Earth and a pronunciation of the Chinese "qi," the life force in all living things.

She ended up as a honeybee (instead of a human girl, as originally planned) because that is what instantly came to mind when I tried to resolve the rhyme for the line, "Which is just how it started with Kee."

Queen Kee

Though not explicitly mentioned 'til much later in the story, there are several places where there are clues that she is a queen. Most notably, in Chapter 1, it mentions she is "neither worker nor drone." That only leaves one thing she can be: queen. See *Queen, Worker, and Drone* in the Science section above.

? It Goes to Eleven!

Yes, parents, this is clearly stolen from *This Is Spinal Tap*. The line in Chapter 1 not only resolves the rhyme nicely, but is also homage to the line from the classic rock and roll movie (Reiner, 1984) where the band declares that unlike inferior rock bands, the volume knob on their amplifier goes all the way to eleven.

CHAPTER 2 - YOU DON'T STINK

Kee's Shear Dare

This is Kee's Shear Dare, the moment when she first addresses her discovery that she's lost a wing, and thus her shot at being queen.

Knowing that the future of a hive depends on a queen's ability to mate, which is typically done in midair, Kee does the noble thing in her departure by setting in motion a natural succession process that allows one of the other budding queens (still in their queen cells) to take over when the next one hatches.

Though she doesn't realize it (nor is it revealed in the story) at the time, her actions are also one of the key steps—the Shear Dare—in dealing with this trauma and transforming the way she sees herself and her future.

The Shear Dare is all about taking control and doing something bold and affirming, which builds confidence and allows you to move on to the more difficult Shed Dare, where the transformation is realized.

Kee's bravery in confronting and winning over Kyle,

a natural predator (she is unaware of his aversion to bees) is her way of taking control. This act will take her on a journey that allows her to discover herself and a way around this issue.

Kyle

Kyle is the name of a wonderful, fun fifteen-year-old boy and good friend who was lost to Muscular Dystrophy (M.D.) in December 2015. Kyle is the younger brother of Ian, another wonderful boy I used to care for at MDA Summer Camp and who was also lost recently to M.D. Kyle and Ian have two amazing younger sisters, Melody and Ellanore, and incredibly brave parents, Rob and Penny.

Kyle is also, of course, the name of Kira's older brother.

Verse to Prose

Yes, this was a conscious—or at least semi-conscious—decision to switch from verse to prose halfway thru this chapter. Symbolically, the transition represents the middle-school transition from childhood to adult—the order and innocence of childhood to the messy, scary, randomness of adulthood.

CHAPTER 3 - ODDBALLS

Unlimited Sting

Unlike workers, the queen does not die after a sting, because her sting (stinger) is unbarbed. She keeps her sting intact and can thus sting many times. Workers, on the other hand, do die afterward. Their sting (stinger) is barbed and becomes lodged in the flesh of the victim, ripping the bottom half of the bee away when removed. Drones (male honeybees) have no stinger (Wilson-Rich, 2014, p. 28).

Super Sniffers

Honeybees have 170 olfactory receptors on their antennae (James E. Kloeppel, 2006), making their sense of smell a hundred times more sensitive than humans (Sammataro & Avitabile, 1998, p. 154).

Won't It Kill You?

In the scene where Kyle is questioning Kee about whether she will die if she stings, Kee seems to have to think about it first. She is obviously bluffing here, going along with the idea that she would die if she stung him. (See Science Note *Unlimited Sting* above). She does not want to give away that she is a queen. She is still a bit ashamed by her perceived inability to fulfill her role in the hive.

The only reasons she has for not stinging at this point are not wanting to hurt Kyle and not divulging her royalty.

CHAPTER 4 - GRUB RUSTLING

Juicy Grub

Skunks, like humans (this human in particular), are omnivores, meaning they will eat anything. They seem to have a special soft spot for juicy beetle larvae (grubs) (Miller, 2015, p. 37).

Bug Musk

Though I have not yet found definitive research that the larval stage of these beetles have a musk smell, the adult brown marmorated stink bug (Halyomorpha halysy) certainly does (Pleasant, 2011). The same could be said of the musk beetle (Aromia moschata), though you would have to go to Europe, North Africa, Asia, or Japan to smell one in person (Step, 1916, pp. 193-196).

Nice Peepers

Honeybees have five eyes, two large compound eyes on the sides, each with 6,900 lenses, and three more eyes, or ocelli as they are called, arranged in a triangle on top (Winston, 1991, pp. 14-15).

CHAPTER 5 - GOO BALL COMETH

Gulp

Snakes, especially rubber boas, are a natural predator of mice (Hoyer, 2001).

Pinky

"Pinky" is the term used for a "feeder mouse," a newborn mouse (typically less than five days old) sold at pet stores as food for snakes. Since they are too young to have a coat of fur, "Pinkies" appear pink in color (What is a Pinkie Mouse?, n.d.).

CHAPTER 6 - THE PACT

Ex-Squeeze Me

Rubber boas are constrictors and kill their prey by squeezing until they have a cardiac arrest (Armitage, 2015).

CHAPTER 7 - RUMBLER TRACKS

My Hive!

More foreshadowing that Kee is probably a queen as she blurts out, "My hive. My hive!" while dreaming. This *is* her hive.

Did You Say Something?

Though we don't know who yells "Kyle" at this point, we will learn that it is Noodles and thus foreshadowing that Noodles can actually speak.

CHAPTER 9 - THE LEGEND OF LUCKY

I Know Your Little Secret

Although Noodles has more than one secret at this point in the story, the one Kyle is referring to is the fact that Noodles can actually talk. Up to this point, they all thought he couldn't. But Kyle is the one who noticed that the only one who could have yelled "Kyle!" when he stepped onto the Rumbler tracks was Noodles. It will be revealed later that Noodles can speak but only chooses to do so when there is something important to say.

Playing Dumb

Noodles pretends to be ignorant and encourages Pinky to talk about Lucky at this point because he wants to see how much of the legend is true and how much has been made up or exaggerated over the years. Noodles knows the original Lucky (Lockie).

At this point, the rest of the characters think there is only one Lucky.

CHAPTER 10 - SANDY'S DINER

Rhus trilobata (Skunkbush)

The sumac bush where Kyle, Pinky, and Noodles briefly hide before sneaking into the diner is also known as the "skunkbush." It can be found in Oregon (where I wrote *Baldilocks and the Three Dares*), California, and the mountains of Idaho and Montana. As you might guess, unlike Kyle, it has no problem emitting a stink, which is how it got its name (Earle & Reveal, 2003).

"Good Grub"

I struggled briefly with the idea that animals could read manmade words—Kyle licking his lips because sign says "Good Grub"—but ultimately went with it. After all, he could also be licking his lips simply because he smells food, and the sign is merely a "humorous" coincidence. And I seem to have no problem with the animals talking and speaking English.

? **My Dear Mom**
Sandy is the name of my dear mother, the amazing, brave, and fun woman who used to chase me around the block with a squirt gun. She also was a cancer sufferer.

? **Chicken Leg #1**
The order that Sally yells back to the kitchen, "Chicken leg #1, on the barbecue," is an homage to a popular song sung each year at Dreamflight by the Duck group. The lyrics go like this...

"Chicken leg, chicken leg, number one
Chicken leg, number two
Chicken leg, chicken leg, number three
Cookin' on the barbecue."

We then sing this verse several times, each time substituting a different food (burger, sausage, etc.)

CHAPTER 11 - ROGUE DRONE

? **Rohan**
Rohan is named after one of the wonderful kids I work with at SNAP (Special Needs Aquatic Program). In *Baldilocks and the Three Dares*, Rohan is the strong, confident, gallant love interest of Kee. Like his namesake, the real Rohan is all of those...or at least the first three. Knowing his charm, I suspect he is not short on classroom suitors.

CHAPTER 12 - SNAKE TALK

Tipsy (Buzzed)

Yes, bees can get tipsy (slightly drunk). Bees some-times consume fermented nectar, which is intoxicating to their system and causes characteristics similar to those of drunk humans—stumbling around, disorientation (can't find their way back to the hive), aggressiveness, and more accidents (flying into stationary objects) (Mingo, 2013, p. 42).

CHAPTER 13 - SHEAR

Have Hive, Will Travel

Hives are often transported via flatbed tractor-trailers to areas needing extra pollinators so that crops will flourish (Jabr, 2013).

CHAPTER 15 - MY HIVE

What Wouldn't I Do?

When Kyle asks Kee what she would do if she could fly again, she responds in verse. As in the beginning of the story, I have used verse whenever a character is in the childhood state of innocence and naiveté, as she is here when she briefly lets her mind wander to thoughts of whimsy and fantasy.

The content of Kee's response is all references to Dreamflight and specifically the Duck group. Each Dream-flight is comprised of 192 kids (along with doctors, nurses, physios, and additional volunteers), split into twelve groups of sixteen. Each group is named after a character from the various Florida theme parks. My group is the Duck group.

"I'd go faster than fast...and higher than high. I'd fly loops upside down and around in the sky," refers to the actual flight itself, a British Airways 747, specially fitted to accommodate the needs of all our kids and their equipment...not to mention an army of medical staff and volunteers.

"I'd go places so far, not like this place at all," refers to the trip from the UK to the USA, a big change for most of these kids.

"With magical Pinkies that grow six feet tall!" is a reference to Mickey Mouse and the Magic Kingdom.

"I'd swim with Duck Lucky...and dolphins, no fear," is a reference to the day when we take the kids to Discovery Cove to swim with dolphins.

"Then bring all I've learned, right back home, to you, here," is a reference to the joy and growth each kid expresses to their family as they return home.

CHAPTER 16 - THE BIG STING

Queen of Queens

As mentioned, queen succession involves the rather unsavory practice of potential new queens killing their sisters in their queen cells (special large, vertical larva cells built specifically to nurture new queens) before they even hatch. In most cases, the first queen to hatch simply goes from queen cell to queen cell and thrusts her stinger inside to kill the competition (Tyson, 2007). In our story, Kee, the first queen to hatch, was immediately attacked by Varroa mites, causing one of her wings to disappear (or become useless). Realizing she cannot fly and is thus unable to fulfill her primary duty as queen—reproducing by mating, in-flight, with drones—she leaves the hive in shame.

CHAPTER 18 - LIFT

Exploding Drones

[WARNING – contains scenes of soon to be mangled male bees]

Yes, drones (male bees) actually explode after successfully mating. This may get a little gross, so be prepared to cringe...or giggle, depending on your age and gender.

Here's the deal. Unlike their female counterparts, male honeybees—drones—do not play a wide variety of roles in the colony. They do not forage for pollen or nectar. They do not build combs for honey storage. They do not guard the hive, and, in fact, do not even have stingers. They do not nurse the brood and they definitely do not help clean. No, drones have but one and only one purpose...to mate.

That may sound like a simple and pain-free job at first, right...if it weren't for one catastrophic detail. If successful, the drone immediately explodes and dies. That's right. After outmaneuvering hundreds of other drones, flying at speeds of up to eighteen miles per hour (Coelho, 1994, p. 22), catching the queen and in midair managing to attach himself, he finally gets the moment he's been waiting for, fertilization, when *BOOM!* Bye-bye bee. His lower abdomen actually explodes, ripping him apart and causing whatever's left of his mangled body to gently fall to earth (Sartell, 2015) (Wilson-Rich, 2014, p. 44). Brutal. But wait, there's more.

If that wasn't disturbing enough for you, this next part should do it. Get your barf bag ready. In order for the next drone to mate with the queen, he has to remove the dismembered parts left behind from the previous drone. Yep. All of a sudden, human puberty doesn't sound so bad.

Strong Women

A primary source of inspiration for *Baldilocks and the Three Dares* has been the incredibly strong women I have run into when dealing with kids with serious health issues. Some of them, like Kira, are the amazingly courageous ones with the health issue, and some, like Kira's mum, are those who have to harness the rock-solid strength and resilience necessary to guide their precious child through the ups and downs of their illness.

Noodles Is Imme

Noodles/Imme did not initially correct Pinky and divulge her true gender partly because Pinky seemed to like the idea of having a guy "buddy," which he never had before. But it also allowed her to conceal and suppress the fact that she was a mother in mourning after losing a child…her adopted duckling, Lockie. It was easier for her to simply go along as the pal of Pinky instead of thinking of being a grieving parent.

Having Noodles initially perceived as male allowed

me to create a classic rambling buddies/three musketeers dynamic for those parts of the story where Kee is missing. Revealing that the strong, silent, protective Noodles is actually a female, and a mother figure at that, allowed me to provide more homage to Aud and the other incredibly brave mothers out there with kids going through health issues.

Imme's Name

Rhyming with "Jimmy," the name Imme comes from a diminutive of Imogen, the name of another beautiful young girl in London who is dealing with cancer. I changed the spelling she uses to "Imme" because it is basically a homograph (same spelling, but different pronunciation and meaning) for "I'm me," Noodles' mantra.

Queen of Everything

Noticing that Kee has surrounded herself with friends that are a skunk, snake, and mouse, Lockie comments that she is not only a queen bee, but is "queen of everything." That is also a phrase we use for Kira.

Sometimes Life Gives You Snake

One of the key points of the story, the expression is first mentioned in Chapter 5 – Goo Ball Cometh, when Pinky describes how he and Noodles first met and was surprised to learn that what seemed like a deadly mistake turned into a symbiotic relationship, something good.

It is referenced again here at the end, when Kee also

confirms that Noodles is not what he seemed—not male—and is, in fact, female and the mother figure, Imme. In both cases, they discover that situations and individuals are not always what they seem. Things or people who may seem scary, foreign, dangerous at first may turn out to be quite the opposite, and even a gift.

Duck Lockie

Yes, "Luckys" do exist, are all around us, and come in all forms from Baldi to duck.

In our story, the first "Lucky" was actually named "Lockie" and is a duck. Thanks to mispronunciation, others who exhibited the qualities of Lockie came to be known as "Lucky."

The important thing for me in developing the concept of "Lucky" was simply to convey the idea that there are real humans out there that possess a level of joy, compassion, bravery, etc. (self-actualization), that cause them to actually radiate those qualities to those around them.

This character is based on an actual little boy named Lockie, currently living in eastern Scotland, and who was one of our wonderful 2013 Dreamflight kids. He was in my group, the "Ducks." Our group seems to have at least one "Lucky" every year. I'll admit, it may be difficult to understand the power of a true "Lucky" without being around one of these amazing kids.

REALLY COOL BOOKS, WEBSITES, AND OTHER STUFF
(BIBLIOGRAPHY)

Armitage, H. (2015, July 22). *Surprise: Snakes don't kill by suffocation.* Retrieved from Science: http://www.sciencemag.org/news/2015/07/surprise-snakes-don-t-kill-suffocation

Coelho, J. R. (1994). *The flight characteristics of drones in relation to mating.* Macomb: Western Illinois University, Department of Biological Sciences.

Earle, A. S., & Reveal, J. L. (2003). *Lewis and Clark's Green World: The Expedition and Its Plants.* Farcountry Press.

Finley, K., & Buford, T. (2016, July 18). Show and Tell with the Owners of Queen Bee Honey Company. (J. Hawley, Interviewer) Corvallis, Oregon.

Honey Bee - Apis mellifera. (n.d.). Retrieved from National Geographic Animals: http://animals.nationalgeographic.com/animals/bugs/honeybee/

Hoyer, R. (2001). *Natural History of the Rubber Boa.* Retrieved from All About The Rubber Boa - Charina bottae: http://www.rubberboas.com/Content/about.html

Jabr, F. (2013, September 1). *The Mind-Boggling Math of Migratory Beekeeping*. Retrieved from Scientific American: https://www.scientificamerican.com/article/migratory-beekeeping-mind-boggling-math/

James E. Kloeppel. (2006, October 25). *Honey bee chemoreceptors found for smell and taste*. Retrieved from University of Illinois: https://news.illinois.edu/blog/view/6367/206824

Miller, A. L. (2015). *Skunk*. Reaktion Books.

Mingo, J. (2013). *Bees Make the Best Pets: All the Buzz About Being Resilient, Collaborative, Industrious, Generous, and Sweet—Straight from the Hive*. Conari Press.

Pleasant, B. (2011, January 17). *Seen Any Brown Marmorated Stink Bugs Lately?* Retrieved from Mother Earth News: http://www.motherearthnews.com/organic-gardening/brown-marmorated-stink-bugs-zb0z11zple

Reiner, R. (Director). (1984). *This is Spinal Tap* [Motion Picture].

Roots, C. (2006). *Nocturnal Animals*. Greenwood Publishing Group.

Sammataro, D., & Avitabile, A. (1998). *The Beekeeper's Handbook.* Cornell University Press.

Sartell, J. (2015, March 30). *Romancing the Queen.* Retrieved from Keeping Backyard Bees: http://www. keepingbackyardbees.com/romancing-the-queen/

Step, E. (1916). *Marvels of Insect Life: A Popular Account of Structure and Habit.* New York: Robert M. McBride & Company.

Tyson, P. (2007, November 7). *Being Queen.* Retrieved from Nova - PBS: http://www.pbs.org/wgbh/nova/ nature/being-queen.html

Webster, T. C. (2013, April). *Kentucky Beekeeping - Entomology.* Retrieved from Entomology at the University of Kentucky: https://entomology.ca.uky. edu/files/efpdf4/ksubeekeeping.pdf

What is a Pinkie Mouse? (n.d.). Retrieved from Animals - mom.me: http://animals.mom.me/ pinkie-mouse-5610.html

Williams, M. (2017, January 10). *The Threat of Varroa Mites: Part 1.* Retrieved from PerfectBee.com: https://www.perfectbee.com/a-healthy-beehive/threats-to-bees/the-threat-and-impact-of-varroa-mites/

Wilson-Rich, N. (2014). *The Bee: A Natural History.*
    (K. Allin, N. Carreck, & A. Quigley, Eds.) Princeton
    University Press.

Winston, M. L. (1991). *The Biology of the Honey Bee.*
    Harvard University Press.

GROUP HUG

Yes, this is the part of the book where I attempt (and fail miserably) to thank all those who generously volunteered or were unceremoniously cajoled, and—when necessary—bribed to help nurture *Baldilocks and the Three Dares* into existence. This is also likely to be the place where—once good—friends and family will repeatedly reference at Thanksgiving and other dinner parties (whatever those are) when I "forget" to mention one or more of them. Be that as it may, let me list those who will now have one less reason to fling the usual scorn and snobbery my way. :)

First, Tricia, best friend and illustrator extraordinaire. You were there for every step, stumble, frustration, and exhilaration along the way. Thanks Noods :@B

Beibei, for the patience and ongoing support and encouragement, even financial help for the summer writing junket that spawned this book. Xiexie ni, hb.

Radhiah Chowdhury for the amazing study notes and blackline masters she created, so we can help teachers use Baldilocks in schools.

All the wonderful friends and family who helped edit, give feedback, or simply put up with my constant book distractions, especially Erin, Jodee, Shawnee, Barbara, Ann, Senta,

Helene, Katie, Yoon, Lynn, and of course Melanie (who, somehow, seems to get all my jokes).

The generous Kathleen Jacoby for the initial pro bono developmental feedback.

My luck in finding such a talented and patient editor in Allister Thompson. You have been so great to work with. Is it supposed to be this fun?! Thank you.

Bonnie and Sean for their generous knowledge, guidance, and sound equipment in the making of the audio book.

Dave Barman and Lito Lopez for their amazing vision and photography skills. It was so much fun working with both of you.

Oregon beekeepers Tad Buford and Karen Finley, who handed me a bee suit and generously took the time to show and tell me some of the basics of how bee colonies work. I am still fascinated.

Pat Pearce for the compassion and energy to cofound Dreamflight and continuing to be a driving force in each year's trip to give 192 kids the holiday of a lifetime. See more about Dreamflight below.

Mitch and Karen for making that call back in 2003 to come to Florida and join Dreamflight. It was right after my mother had died from cancer, so it was exactly what was needed. It changed my life and is still doing so.

Kira, Aud, and family for showing us all what bravery and family support truly means, and of course for inspiring me to write this book. See more about Kira below.

And last but not least, location, location, location…and

the two wonderful relatives who made it possible. If it were not for a beautiful little piece of farmland in central Oregon, I am not sure this book would have become the story it did… or happen at all. It is amazing what sitting under an apple tree and talking to cows for eight hours a day will do for your plots and characters. This was supposed to be a thirty-two-page children's picture book.

I owe a huge thanks to my wonderful Aunt Barby and hilarious Uncle Dave, who allowed me to invade their little piece of paradise and squat on the farm for six weeks. Thank you so much for everything. See you this summer for the next book. :)

Dreamflight

Dreamflight is an amazing organization that takes kids with serious illnesses or disabilities on a ten-day journey of fun and self-discovery—one that pushes boundaries, empowers, and builds self-esteem. Overwhelming, exciting, exhausting. Laughter, tears. Life-long friends, *life-changing*. That is Dreamflight.

I became involved with Dreamflight in 2003, when my good friend Karen called me from Florida and said her husband, Mitch, was involved in an amazing charity for kids that I might be interested in. Mitch warned me it would be addictive. They were both right.

Kira

Kira, who turned fourteen in June, is one of the bravest, most compassionate, and fun-loving humans you will ever meet…and she just happens to be in the midst of tackling a mean case of neuroblastoma.

In pure Kira fashion, she has dealt with it by confronting each challenge head-on with determination, humor, and her infectious, ever-present smile. Instead of letting the effects of chemotherapy dictate when and where her lovely locks would depart, she took control, shaved her head, and proudly displayed that beautiful, bald noggin for all to see…smiling the whole time.

If Kira can dare to take on the incredibly daunting challenges associated with cancer, the rest of us can certainly show our solidarity by taking on a few dares of our own. Thus was born the idea for *Baldilocks and the Three Dares*.

I met Kira at the 2015 Dreamflight trip when she was part of the Ducks, the best group ever!

ABOUT
THE AUTHOR AND ILLUSTRATOR

Jimothy Newton

Born on a peanut farm in the shady side of Forenzy Trough, I came to writing children's fiction via the usual path—a degree in electrical engineering, followed by fifteen years of mind-numbing software development. Though new to publishing, I am not at all new to storytelling nor the haphazard, immature—if not scatological—musings of the preteen mind. I have worked with and around the little beasties since I first became one myself.

This is my first book (so be gentle). *Baldilocks* was inspired by the courageous, compassionate, and just plain fun kids I have had the honor to know and work with over the years thru Dreamflight (dreamflight.org), MDA (mda.org), and SNAP (snapkids.org).

Oh…and there is no peanut farm nor Forenzy Trough. I was born on a standard, quarter-acre, 1960s-era ranch-house lot in sunny, Concord, California. And Jimothy Newton—also not real. Jimothy is a nickname and Newton is taken from the most famous Newton of all—Fig Newton. So when it came time to put a name on my first book for kids, it was no contest. I mean really—which one sounds more fun to cut class and hang out with (something I am definitely NOT recommending…necessarily), Jimothy Newton or James Edwin Hawley? Exactly. Now go back to class.

Tricia Seibold

Tricia Seibold spent countless hours of her childhood perched in her favorite tree, drawing and dreaming up ways to make art her job. Her favorite art teacher saw potential and helped her figure out how to make it happen (and convince her parents it was actually a good idea). After earning her BFA, Tricia began her career designing toy and candy packaging before moving on to publishing, where she served as the art director at *Communication Arts* magazine for thirteen years. She has since enjoyed a successful freelance design career, where she occasionally gets to exercise her illustration muscles for client work. She is grateful every single day that people actually PAY her to do what she loves.

START HERE

1

2

DUCK FORCE
ONE

Tear-out (shhhh!)
Paper Airplane

Yes! You get to tear
a page out of a book!
Woo Hoo!

3

FOLD
BACK

FOLD
BACK

QUACK!

QUACK!

QUACK!

QUACK!

Baldilocks3Dares.org

Facebook.com/groups/baldilocks3dares

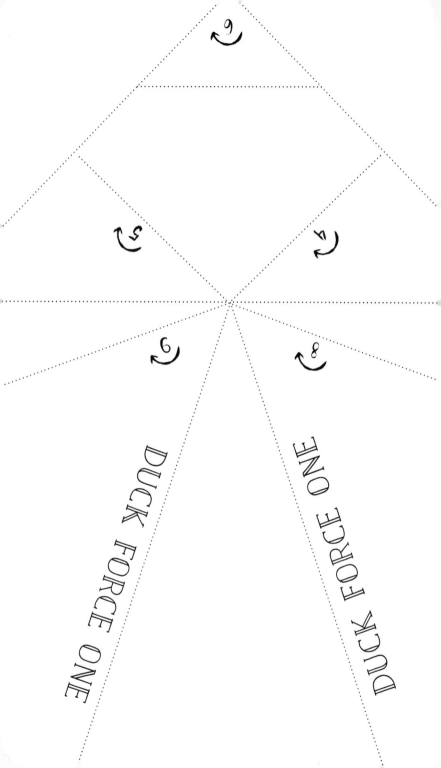

9

5

7

6

8

DUCK FORCE ONE

DUCK FORCE ONE

25395880R00090

Printed in Great Britain
by Amazon